The German Lieutenant And Other Stories

by

August Strindberg

Double9 BOOKS

The German Lieutenant And Other Stories
by August Strindberg

ISBN: 978-93-61422-13-3

Published by

DOUBLE 9 BOOKS
2/13-B, Ansari Road
Daryaganj, New Delhi – 110002
info@double9books.com
www.double9books.com
Tel. 011-40042856

ABOUT THE AUTHOR

Johan August Strindberg was a Swedish dramatist, novelist, poet, essayist, and painter. During his four-decade career, Strindberg created more than sixty plays and over thirty books of fiction, autobiography, history, cultural analysis, and politics, frequently drawing directly on his own experiences. He was a daring innovator and iconoclast who experimented with a variety of dramatic methods and objectives, including naturalistic tragedy, monodrama, and history plays, as well as his foreshadowing of expressionist and surrealist theatrical tactics. Strindberg pioneered new approaches to dramatic action, vocabulary, and visual composition beginning with his early work. In 1872, the Royal Theatre rejected his first major play, Master Olof; it was not until 1881, at the age of thirty-two, that its premiere at the New Theatre provided him with his theatrical breakthrough. In his plays The Father (1887), Miss Julie (1888), and Creditors (1889), he created naturalistic dramas that - building on the established accomplishments of Henrik Ibsen's prose problem plays while rejecting their use of the structure of the well-made play - responded to Emile Zola's manifesto "Naturalism in the Theatre" (1881) and the example set by André Antoine's newly established Théâtre Libre (opened 1887).

CONTENTS

THE GERMAN LIEUTENANT

CHAPTER I

It was fourteen days after Sedan, in the middle of September, 1870. A former clerk in the Prussian Geological Survey, later a lieutenant in the reserve, named Von Bleichroden, sat in his shirt-sleeves before a writing-table in the Café du Cercle, the best inn of the little town Marlotte. He had thrown his military coat with its stiff collar over the back of a chair, and there it hung limp, and collapsed like a corpse, with its empty arms seeming to clutch at the legs of the chair to keep itself from falling headlong. Round the body of the coat one saw the mark of the sword-belt, and the left coat-tail was rubbed quite smooth by the sheath. The back of the coat was as dusty as a high-road, and the lieutenant-geologist might have studied the tertiary deposits of the district on the edges of his much-worn trousers. When the orderlies came into the room with their dirty boots, he could till by the traces they left on the floor whether they had been walking over Eocene or Pleiocene formations. He was really more a geologist than a soldier, but for the present he was a letter-writer. He had pushed his spectacles up to his forehead, sat with his pen at rest, and looked out of the window.

The garden lay in all its autumn glory before him, and the branches of the apple and pear trees bent with a load of the most splendid fruit to the ground. Orange-red pumpkins sunned themselves close beside prickly grey-green artichokes; fiery-red tomatoes clambered up sticks near wool-white cauliflowers; sun-flowers as large as a plate were turning their yellow disks towards the west, where the sun was beginning to sink; whole companies of dahlias, white as fresh-starched linen, purple-red like congealed blood, dirty-red like fresh-slaughtered flesh, salmon-red, sulphur-yellow, flax-coloured, mottled and speckled, sang one great flower-concert. Then there was the sand-strewn path lined by two rows of giant gilly-flowers; faintly lilac-coloured, dazzlingly ice-blue, and straw-yellow, they continued the perspective to where the vineyards stood in their brownish-green array, a small wood of thyrsus-staves with the reddened grape-clusters half hidden under the leaves. Behind them were the whitening, unharvested stalks of the cornfields, with the over-ripe ears of corn hanging sorrowfully towards the ground, with wide-open husks and bractlets at every gust of wind paying their tribute to the earth and bursting with their juices. And far in the background were the oak-tree tops and the beechen arches of the Forest of Fontainebleau, whose outlines melted away into the finest denticulations, like old Brussels lace, into the extreme meshes of which the horizontal rays of the evening sun wove gold threads. Some bees were still visiting the splendid honey-flowers in the garden; a robin-redbreast twittered in an apple tree; strong gusts of scent came now and then from the gilly-flowers, as when one walks along a pavement and the door of a scent-shop is opened.

The lieutenant sat with his pen at rest, visibly entranced by the beautiful scene. "What a lovely land!" he thought, and his recollection went back to the sandy plain of his home, diversified by some wretched stunted firs which stretched their gnarled arms towards the sky as though they implored the favour of not having to drown in the sand.

But the beautiful landscape which was framed in the window was shadowed as regularly as clockwork by the musket of the sentry, whose bright, shining bayonet bisected the picture, and who turned on his rounds exactly under a pear tree heavily laden with the finest yellow-green Napoleon pears.

The lieutenant thought for a moment of asking him to choose another beat, but did not venture to do so; so in order to escape the flash of the bayonet, he let his gaze wander to the left over the courtyard. There stood the cook-house with its yellow-plastered wall, and an old knotty vine spread out against it like the skeleton of some animal in a museum; the vine was without leaves or clusters, and it stood there as though crucified, nailed fast to the decaying espalier, stretching out its long tough arms and fingers as though it wished to draw the sentry into its ghostly embrace as he turned.

The lieutenant turned away and looked at his writing-table. There lay the unfinished letter to his young wife whom he had married four months previously, two months before the war broke out. Beside his field-glass and the list of the French General Staff lay Hartmann's "Philosophy of the Unconscious" and Schopenhauer's "Parerga and Paralipomena." Suddenly he rose from the table and walked up and down the room. It had been the meeting and dining-room of the artists' colony which had now vanished. The wainscoting of the walls was adorned with little oil-paintings recording happy hours in the beautiful hospitable country which so generously opened its art-schools and its exhibitions to foreigners. Here were depicted Spanish dancing-women, Roman monks, scenes from the coasts of Normandy and Brittany, Dutch wind-mills, Scandinavian fishing-villages and Swiss Alps.

Into one corner had crept an easel of walnut-wood, and seemed to be hiding itself in the shadow from some threatening bayonets. A palette smeared with half-dried colours hung there and looked like a liver hanging in a pork-shop. Some red Spanish militia caps belonging to the painters, with the colour half faded by exposure to the sun and rain, hung on the clothes-horse.

The lieutenant felt embarrassed, like one who has intruded into a stranger's house, and expects the owner to come and surprise him. He therefore abruptly ceased walking up and down and took his seat at the table in order to continue his letter. He had finished the first pages, which were full of expressions of his sorrow, home-sickness and anxiety since he had lately heard news which confirmed his joyful hopes of becoming a father. He dipped his pen in the ink rather in order to have someone to talk with than to give or ask for news. He wrote as follows:

"So, for example, when I with my hundred men after a march of fourteen hours without food or water, came to a wood where we found an abandoned provision-wagon, what do you think happened? So famished that their eyes protruded from their heads like mountain crystals in granite, the body of men broke up and threw themselves like wolves upon the food, and since there was scarcely enough for twenty-five, they came to blows. No one listened to my word of command, and when the sergeant struck them with the flat of his sabre, they knocked him down with the butt-ends of their muskets. Sixteen men remained wounded and half dead on the place. Those who got hold of the food ate so greedily that they became sick and had to lie down on the ground, where they at once fell asleep. They fought with their own countrymen like wild beasts who fight for food.

"One day we received orders to throw up defences. In the unwooded tract of country we were in there was nothing to use but the vines and their stakes. It was a strange sight to see how the vineyards were rifled in an hour—how the vine-stems were torn up, together with the leaves and grapes, to form faggot-bundles, which were quite wet with the juice of the crushed, half-ripe grapes. It was said that the vines were forty years old. Thus we destroyed the work of forty years in an hour. And that too in order to shoot down those who had provided the material for the faggot-bundles which protected us!

"Another day we had to skirmish in an unreaped field of corn where the ears of corn dropped round our feet like hail and the stalks were trodden down to rot at the next shower of rain. Do you think, my dear wife, that one can sleep quietly at night after such doings? And yet, what have I done but my duty? And people venture to assert that the consciousness of duty performed is the best pillow for one's head.

"But there are still worse things behind. You have perhaps heard that the French population in order to strengthen their army have risen in a mass and formed bodies of volunteers, who, under the name of 'franc-tireurs,' try to protect their farms and fields. The Prussian Government has refused to recognise them as soldiers, but has threatened to have them shot down as spies and traitors whenever they are found; because, they say, it is states who wage war and not individuals. But are soldiers not individuals? And are not these franc-tireurs soldiers? They have a grey uniform like the chasseur regiments, and uniforms make soldiers. But it is objected that they are not registered. No, they are not registered, because the Government has neither had time to have it done nor are means of communication with the country districts so easy as to make it possible. I have just got three of these franc-tireurs prisoners in the billiard-room, and am every moment expecting orders from headquarters to decide their fate."

Here he stopped writing, and rang for his orderly.

The latter, who was in waiting in the tap-room, at once appeared in the dining-room before the lieutenant.

"How are the prisoners going on?" asked Von Bleichroden.

"Very well, sir; they are just now playing billiards, and are quite cheerful."

"Give them some bottles of wine, but of the weakest kind. Has nothing happened?"

"Nothing, sir."

Von Bleichroden continued his letter.

"What strange people these Frenchmen are! The three franc-tireurs whom I have just mentioned, and who possibly (I say possibly for I still hope for the best) may be condemned to death in a few days, are just now playing billiards in the room next to mine and I hear their cues striking the balls. What happy contempt of the world! It is really splendid to go hence in such a mood; or rather, it shows that life is worth very little if one can part from it so easily—I mean when one has not such dear ties binding one to existence as I possess. Of course you won't misunderstand me and believe that I think I am tied— — Ah! I don't know what I am writing, for I have not slept for several nights and my head is so— —"

Just then there was a knock at the door.

At the lieutenant's "Come in!" the door opened and the curé of the village entered. He was a man of about fifty, with a friendly and melancholy yet firm expression of face.

"I come, sir," he began, "to ask you for permission to speak with the prisoners."

The lieutenant rose and put on his coat, while he offered the curé a seat on the sofa. But when he had buttoned up the coat tightly and felt the stiff collar close round his neck, it seemed as though his nobler organs were compressed, and as though his blood stood still in coursing through secret channels to his heart. Placing his hand on the copy of Schopenhauer, and leaning against the writing-table, he said: "I am at your service, Monsieur le Curé, but I do not think the prisoners will pay you much attention, for they are busy playing billiards."

"I think, sir," answered the curé, "that I know my people better than you do. One question. Do you intend to have these young fellows shot?"

"Naturally," answered Von Bleichroden, quite prepared to assume his rôle. "It is the states which wage war, Monsieur le Curé, not individuals."

"Pardon me, sir, are you and your soldiers not individuals?"

"Pardon me, Monsieur, not for the present."

He slipped the letter to his wife under the blotting-paper and continued, "I am just now only a representative of the German Confederation of States."

"But, sir, your amiable Empress, whom may God ever protect, was also a representative of the German Confederation when she issued her proclamation to German women to help the wounded, and I know of hundreds of individual Frenchmen who bless her, although the French nation curses your nation. Sir, in the name of Jesus the Redeemer" (here the curé stood up, seized his enemy's hands and continued in a tear-choked voice), "could you not appeal to her?"

The lieutenant was nearly losing his self-control, but he recovered himself and said: "With us women have not yet begun to interfere in politics."

"That is a pity," answered the priest, and stood up.

The lieutenant seemed to have heard a noise through the window, so that he did not pay attention to the priest's answer. He became restless, and his face was quite white, for the stiff collar could no longer prevent the blood quitting it.

"Pray sit down, Monsieur," he said. "If you wish to speak with the prisoners, you can do so, but remain sitting for a minute." (He listened out of the window again, and now there were heard distinctly doubled hoof-beats, as of a horse galloping.) "No, don't go, Monsieur," he said with a gasp. The sound of galloping came nearer till it became a walk, slackened and ceased. There was the clinking of a sword and spurs, footsteps, and Von Bleichroden held a letter in his hand. He tore it open and read it.

"What is the time?" he asked himself. "Six! In two hours, Monsieur, the prisoners will be shot without trial."

"Impossible, sir! One does not so hurry men into eternity."

"Eternity or not, the order says that it must be done before vespers, if I do not wish to regard myself as making common cause with the franc-tireurs. And here there follows a sharp reprimand because I have not carried out the order of August 31st. Monsieur, go in and talk with them and spare me the unpleasantness."

"You think it unpleasant to report a righteous sentence?"

"But I am still a man, Monsieur! Don't you think I am a man?"

He tore open his coat to get air, and began to walk up and down the room.

"Why cannot we be always men? Why must we have two faces? Oh, Monsieur, go in and talk with them! Are they married men? Have they wives and children—parents perhaps?"

"They are all three unmarried," answered the priest. "But at any rate you might let them have this one night."

"Impossible! The order says, 'before vespers,' and we have to march at daybreak. Go to them, Monsieur, go to them!"

"I will go; but remember, Mr Lieutenant, not to go out in your shirt-sleeves, when you go, or you might meet with the same fate as they. For it is the coat, you know, which makes the soldier."

And the priest went.

Von Bleichroden wrote the last lines of his letter in a state of great agitation. Then he sealed it and rang for the orderly.

"Post this letter," he said to him, "and send in the sergeant."

The sergeant came.

"Three times three is twenty-nine—no, three times seven is. Sergeant, take three times—take seven-and-twenty men and shoot the prisoners within an hour. Here is the order!"

"Shoot them?" asked the sergeant hesitatingly.

"Yes, shoot them! Choose the worst soldiers, those who have been under fire before. You understand? For instance, number 86, Besel, number 19, Gewehr, and so on. Order also for me a fatigue-party of sixteen men at once, and choose the best. We will make a reconnaissance towards Fontainebleau, and when we come back it will be over. Do you understand?"

"Sixteen men for you, air, and seven-and-twenty for the prisoners. God protect you, sir!"

And he went.

The lieutenant buttoned his coat again carefully, put on his sword-belt, and placed a revolver in his pocket. Then he lit a cigar, but found it impossible to smoke for he had not enough air in his lungs. He dusted his writing-table; he took his handkerchief and wiped the large pair of scissors, the stick of sealing-wax, and the match-box; he laid the ruler and the pen-holder parallel at an exact right angle with the blotting-paper; then he began to put the furniture straight. When that was finished, he took out his brush and comb and did his hair before the looking-glass; he took down the palette and examined the dabs of paint on it; he inspected all the red caps and tried to make the easel stand on two legs. By the time that the clanking of the weapons of his fatigue-party was audible in the courtyard, there was not a single object in the room which he had not handled.

Then he went out, gave the command "Left wheel! March!" and quitted the village.

He felt as though he were running away from a foe of superior power, and the soldiers found it difficult to follow him. When they came to a field he made them go in single file so as not to trample down the grass. He did not turn round, but the soldier next behind him could see how the cloth of the back of his coat twitched from time to time, as when one shudders, or expects a blow from behind.

At the edge of the wood he ordered a halt; he told the men to keep quiet and to rest while he went into the wood. When he found himself alone and was quite sure that no one could see him, he took a deep breath and turned towards the dark thickets through which narrow foot-paths lead to the Gorge-aux-loups. The under-wood and bushes lay in shadow, but above the sun still shone brightly on the tops of the oaks and beeches. He felt as though he lay on the dark bottom of the sea, and through the green water saw above him the light of day which he never more would reach. The great, wonderfully beautiful wood which formerly had soothed his troubled spirit seemed this evening so disharmonious, so repellent, so cold. Life appeared so heartless, so contradictory, and Nature herself seemed unhappy in her unconscious sleep. Here also the terrible struggle for existence was being carried on, bloodlessly it is true, but just as cruelly as by conscious creatures. He saw how the baby oaks spread themselves out to bushes in order to kill the tender beech-seedlings which would never be more than seedlings; of a thousand beeches only one could get to the light and thereby become a giant, which should in its turn rob the rest of life. And the ruthless oak, which stretched out its gnarled, rough arms as though it wished to keep the whole sun for itself, had discovered how to wage an underground strife. It sent out its long roots in all directions, undermining the ground; it ate away from the others the smallest particles of nourishment; and when it could not overshadow a rival till it was dead, it starved it out. The oak had already murdered the pine-wood, but the beech came as an avenger slow but sure, for its acrid juices kill everything where it predominates. It had discovered the method of poisoning which was irresistible, for not a single plant could grow in-its shadow; the earth around it was dark as a grave, and therefore the future belonged to it.

The lieutenant wandered on and on. He struck about with his sword without thinking how many hopeful young oaklings he destroyed, how many headless cripples he produced. In fact he hardly thought any more, for all the activities of his soul seemed crushed in a mortar to pulp. His thoughts tried to crystallise themselves but dissolved and floated away; memories, hopes, wrath, gentler feelings, and one great hatred of all the perversity which by the operation of an inexplicable natural force had come to rule the world, melted together in his brain, as though an inner fire had suddenly raised the temperature and obliged all its solid constituents to assume a fluid form.

Suddenly he started and stood still as if arrested, for from Marlotte came a sound rolling over the fields and redoubling its echoes in the hollow passage of the "Wolves' gorge." It was the drum! First a long roll—trrrrrrrrrrrrom!—and then blow on blow, one and two, dull and muffled, as when one nails up a coffin and fears to disturb the house of mourning—trrrom!—trrrom!—trom!—trom!

He took out his watch; it was a quarter to seven. In a quarter of an hour it would happen! He wished to return and see it. No, he had just run away to avoid it; he would not see it for anything. Then he climbed up a tree.

Now he saw the village, which looked so bright and homelike with its little gardens and church-tower rising above the house roofs. He saw no more, but held his watch in his hand and followed the second hand. Tick, tick, tick, tick—it ran round the little dial-plate so swiftly; but when the second hand had made one round, the long one made a jerk and the steady hour hand stood still, as it seemed to him, though it was moving also.

Now the watch showed five minutes to seven. He gripped the smooth black beech stem he was standing by very tightly. The watch trembled in his hand, there was a humming in his ears, and he felt a burning sensation at the roots of his hair. Crash! There was a sound just as when a plank breaks, and above a dark slate roof and a white apple tree rose a blue cloud of smoke over the village, bluish white like a spring cloud; but above the cloud one, two, and several smoke-rings shot up in the air, as though they had been shooting at pigeons and not towards a wall.

"They were not all so bad as I thought," he said to himself as he got down from the tree, feeling quieter now that it was over. And now the little village church bell began to ring, speaking of peace and quiet for the dead who had done their duty, but not for all the living who had done theirs.

The sun had gone down, and the moon, whose pale yellow disk had hung in the sky all the afternoon, began to redden and gather light as the lieutenant with his men marched by Montcourt, still followed by the ringing of the little bell. They came out on the great high-road to Nemours, which, with its two rows of poplars, seemed peculiarly suited for marching on. So they went on till it was quite night and the moon shone clearly. In the last row the men had already begun to whisper and consult secretly whether they should not ask the corporal to give the lieutenant some sort of hint that the district was unsafe and that they should return to their quarters in order to be able to march at daybreak, when Von Bleichroden quite unexpectedly commanded "Halt!" They stood on a rising ground from which Marlotte could be seen.

The lieutenant stood quite still, like a pointer who startles a covey of partridges. Now the drum was beating again. Then the clock in Montcourt struck nine, followed by those in Grez, in Bourron, in Nemours; and then all the little church bells began to ring for vespers, vying with each other in shrillness, and through them all pierced the tones of the bell in Marlotte, which called "Help! help!" and Von Bleichroden could not help. Now came a booming along the ground, as though from the depths of the earth; it was the firing of the evening gun at the headquarters in Chalons. The moon shone through the light evening mists which were lying like great flocks of wool above the little River Loin, and lit it up so that it resembled a lava stream running in the distance from the dark wood of Fontainebleau which rose like a volcano. The evening was oppressively warm, but the men had all white faces, so that the bats which swarmed around them flew close by their ears, as they do when they see anything white. All knew what the lieutenant was thinking about, but they had never seen him behave so strangely and feared that it was not all right with this aimless reconnaissance on the high-road. At last the corporal summoned up boldness to approach him, and under the form of making a report drew his attention to the fact that the tattoo had sounded.

Von Bleichroden received the information with a humble air, as when one receives a command, and gave the order to return home.

When, one hour later, they entered the first street of Marlotte the corporal noticed that the lieutenant's right leg was contracted as though by a spavin, and that he moved in a diagonal course like a horse-fly. In the market-place the troops were dismissed without evening prayers, and the lieutenant disappeared.

He did not wish to return to his rooms at once. Something was drawing him he knew not whither. He ran about with widely opened eyes and inflated nostrils, like a hound on the scent. He examined the walls and sniffed for a familiar smell. He saw nothing and met no one. He wished to see where "it" had happened, but he also feared to see it. At last he became tired and went home. In the courtyard he stopped and then went round the cook-house. Suddenly he came upon the sergeant and was so startled that he had to support himself by holding on to the wall. The sergeant was also startled, but recovered himself and began, "I was looking for you, sir, in order to make my report."

"Very good! Very good indeed! Go home and lie down," answered Von Bleichroden, as though he feared to hear details.

"Yes, sir, but it was——"

"Very good! Go! Go!"

He spoke so quickly and uninterruptedly that it was impossible for the sergeant to put in a word. Every time he opened his mouth he was overwhelmed with a torrent of words, so that at last he became tired of it and went away. Then the lieutenant breathed again and felt like a boy who has escaped a thrashing.

He was now in the garden. The moon shone brightly on the yellow wall of the cook-house, and the vine stretched its skeleton arms as though in a very long yawn. But what was that? Two or three hours before it had been dead and leafless, simply a grey skeleton which writhed, and now were there not hanging on it the finest red clusters, and had not the stem grown green? He went nearer in order to see whether it was the same vine.

As he came close to the wall he stepped in something slippery and was aware of the same nauseous smell which one perceives in butchers' shops. And now he saw that it was the same vine, certainly the same, but the plaster of the wall was broken by bullets and sprinkled with blood.

He went away quickly. When he came into the front hall he stumbled over something which lay under his feet. He drew off his boots in the hall and threw them out in the garden. Then he went into his room, where his tea was laid. He felt terribly hungry but could not eat. He remained standing and staring at the covered table which was so neatly spread: the white pat of butter with a little radish laid on the top of it; the tablecloth was white and he saw that it was embroidered with his or his wife's initials, which had not been there at first; the little goat's milk cheese lay so neatly on its vine leaf, as though something more than the fear of a forced contribution had operated here; the beautiful little white loaf so unlike the brown rye-bread to which he was accustomed; the red wine in the polished decanter; the thin reddish slices of mutton—all seemed to have been arranged by friendly hands. But he felt afraid to touch the food, and suddenly rang the bell. Immediately the landlady stood in the doorway without saying a word. She looked down at his feet and waited for an order. The lieutenant did not know what he wanted, nor did he remember for what he had rung, but he had to say something.

"Are you angry with me?" he stammered.

"No, sir," answered the woman mildly. "Does the gentleman want anything?" And she looked down again at his feet.

He also looked down to see what had attracted her attention, and discovered that he was standing in his stockings, and that the floor was covered with red footprints—red footprints with the mark of the toes where his stockings had been torn, for he had walked far that day.

"Give me your hand, my good woman," he said, stretching out his own.

"No," answered the woman, and looked straight into his eyes. Then she left the room.

Herr von Bleichroden tried to pluck up courage after this snub, and took a chair and sat down to his meal. He lifted the plate of meat in order to help himself, but the smell of the meat made him feel ill. He stood up, opened the window, and threw the whole plate with its contents into the garden. His whole body trembled and he felt sick; his eyes were so sensitive that the light tried them, and all bright colours irritated them. He threw out the red bottle of wine, he took away the red radish from the butter, the red painters' caps and palettes—everything that was red had to go. Then he lay down on the bed. His eyes were tired, but he could not close them, so he lay for an hour, till he heard voices in the tap-room. He did not wish to listen, but he could not shut his ears, and recognised that they were two corporals who were drinking beer and talking.

"Those were two sturdy fellows—the two short ones, but the long one was weak."

"Yes, he fell like a bundle of rags by the wall. He had asked that they should fasten him to the espalier, for he wished to stand, he said."

"But the others—devil take me!—stood with their arms folded over their breasts, as though they were going to be photographed."

"Yes, but when the priest came into the billiard-room and told them there was no chance, all three fell crash on the ground, so at least the sergeant said, but there was no scream nor prayer for mercy."

"Yes, they were deuced plucky chaps. Your health!"

Herr von Bleichroden pressed his head into his pillow and stopped his ears with the sheets. But presently he got up. It was as if something drew him forcibly to the door behind which they were talking, he wanted to hear more; but the corporals now conversed in low tones. Accordingly he stole forward, leant his back against a corner, laid his ear to the keyhole and listened.

"But did you see our people? Their faces were as grey as pipe ashes, and many of them shot in the air. Don't let us talk more about it! But they got what they deserved, and they weighed much more when they went than when they came. It was like shooting little birds with grapeshot."

"Did you see the priest's boys in red cassocks who stood and sang with the coffee-roasters? It was like snuffing out a light when the rifles cracked. They rolled in the bean-beds like sparrows, fluttering their wings and turning their eyes. And how the old women came and picked up the pieces! Oh! oh! but so it goes in war. Your health!"

Herr von Bleichroden had heard enough; the blood had so gone to his brain that he could not sleep. He went into the tap-room and told the corporals-to go home. Then he undressed himself, dipped his head in the hand-basin, took up Schopenhauer and began to read with pulses beating violently:

"Birth and death both belong to life; they constitute two opposites which condition each other; they are the two extreme poles in each manifestation of life. This is just what the deepest of all mythologies, the Hindu, has expressed by investing Siva the goddess of destruction with a necklace of skulls and the Lingam, the organ of reproduction. Death is the painful dissolution of a knot which was tied in pleasure, it is the forcible doing away with the fundamental mistake of our existence, it is deliverance from a delusion."

He let the book drop, for he heard someone crying and tossing about in his bed. Who was in the bed? He saw a body, the under part of which was painfully contorted by cramp, while the muscles of the chest stood out strained like the staves of a cask, and he heard a low, hollow sound like a shriek smothered under the bed-clothes. It was his own body! Had he then been divided into two, that he heard and saw himself as though he were another person? The screaming continued. The door opened and the mild-mannered landlady came in, probably alter knocking.

"What does the gentleman want?" she asked with shining eyes and a peculiar smile upon her lips.

"I!" answered the sick man. "Nothing! But I am very ill and would like to see a doctor."

"There is no doctor here, but the priest is accustomed to help us," answered the woman, smiling no longer.

"Send for the priest then," said the lieutenant, "though I don't generally like them."

"But when one is ill, one likes them," said the woman, and disappeared.

When the priest entered he went to the bed and took the sick man's wrist.

"What do you think it is?" asked the latter. "What do you think it is?"

"A bad conscience," was the priest's brief reply.

Herr von Bleichroden answered excitedly, "A bad conscience after doing one's duty!"

"Yes," answered the priest, tying a wet handkerchief round the sick man's head. "Listen to me while you still can. It is now *you* who are condemned—to a worse lot than the —three! Listen to me carefully. I know the symptoms. You are on the edge of madness. You must try to think the matter out. Think hard, and you will find your brain get right again. Look at me, and follow my words if you can. You have become two persons. You regard one part of yourself as though it were a second or a third person. How did that happen? It is the social falsehood, which makes us all double. When you wrote to your wife to-day you were a man—a true, simple, good man; but when you spoke with me you were another character altogether. Just as an actor loses his personality and becomes a mere conglomeration of the parts he performs, so an official becomes two persons at least. Now when there comes a spiritual shock, upheaval or earthquake, the soul splits, as it were, in two, and the two natures lie side by side, and contemplate each other.

"I see a book lying on the ground which I also know. The author was a deep thinker, perhaps the deepest of all. He saw through the misery and nothingness of earthly life as though he had learnt from our Lord and Saviour, but for all that he could not help being a double character, for life, birth, habit and human weakness compelled him to relapses. You see, sir, that I have read other books beside the breviary. And I talk as a doctor, not as a priest, for we both—follow me carefully—we both understand one another. Do you think I do not know the curse of the double life which I lead? Not that I feel any doubt of the holy things, which have passed into my blood and bones, so to speak, but I know, sir, that I do not speak in God's name when I speak. Falsehood passes into us from our mother's womb and breast, and he who would tell the whole truth out under present circumstances—yes, yes! Can you follow me?"

The sick man listened eagerly, and his eyelids had not dropped once all the time the priest was speaking.

"Now there is a little traitor," continued the priest, "with a torch in his hand, an angel who goes about with a basket of roses with which he bestrews the refuse-heaps of life. He is an angel of deceit, and he is called 'The Beautiful.' The heathen worshipped him in Greece; princes have done him homage, for he has bewitched the eyes of people so that they could not see things as they are. He goes through the whole of life, falsifying and falsifying. Why do you warriors dress in splendid clothes with gold and brilliant colours? Why do you always work with music and flying flags? Is it not to conceal what is really at the bottom of your profession? If you loved the truth, you ought to go about in white smocks, like butchers, so that the bloodstains might show distinctly, with knives and marrow-borers as they do in slaughter-houses, with axes dripping blood and greasy with tallow. Instead of a band of music, you ought to drive before you a herd of howling maniacs whom the sights of the battlefield have driven crazy; instead of flags, you should carry shrouds and draw coffins on your wagon-trains." The sick man, who now writhed in convulsions, clasped his hands in prayer and bit his finger-nails. The priest's face had assumed a terrible expression—hard, implacable, hostile. He continued:

"You are naturally a good man, you, and I will not punish that side of you, but I punish you as a representative, as you called yourself, and your punishment will be a warning to others. Will you see the three corpses? Will you see them?"

"No! For Jesus' sake!" shrieked the sick man, whose nightshirt was wet with sweat and clung to his shoulder-blades.

"Your cowardice shows that you are a man, and, as such, cowardly."

As though struck by the blow of a whip, the sick man started up; his face seemed composed, his chest was no more convulsed, and with a calm voice, as though he were quite well, he said: "Go, devil of a priest, or you will make me do something desperate."

"But I shall not come again if you call me," said the other. "Remember that! Remember, that if you cannot sleep it is not my fault, but the fault of those who lie in the billiard-room! In the billiard-room, you know!" He flung open the door of the billiard-room, and a terrible smell of carbolic acid streamed into the sick-chamber. "Do you smell it? Do you smell it? That is not like smelling powder, nor is it an exploit to telegraph home about. Great victory! Three dead and one mad! God be praised! It is not an occasion for writing odes, strewing flowers in the streets, and singing Te Deums in the churches? It is not a victory! It is murder, murder, you murderer!"

Herr von Bleichroden had sprung out of bed and jumped out of the window. In the courtyard he was seized by some of his men, whom he tried to bite. Then he was bound and placed in a headquarter ambulance in order to be taken to the asylum as a complete maniac.

CHAPTER II

It was a sunny morning at the end of February, 1871. Up the steep Martheray Hill in Lausanne a young woman walked slowly, leaning on the arm of a middle-aged man. She was far gone in pregnancy, and hung heavily on her companion's arm. Her face was that of a girl, but it was pale with care, and she was dressed in mourning. The man was not, from which the passers-by concluded that he was not her husband. He seemed in deep trouble, stooped down now and then to the little woman and said a word or two to her, then seemed to be absorbed again in his own thoughts. When they came to the old custom-house in front of the inn "A l'Ours," they stood still.

"Is there another hill?" she asked.

"Yes, dear," he answered. "Let us sit down for a moment."

They sat down on a seat before the inn. Her heart beat slowly and her breast heaved painfully, as though for want of air.

"I am sorry for you, poor brother," she said. "I see that you are longing to be with your own family."

"Don't mention it, sister! Don't let us talk about it. Certainly my heart is sometimes far away, and they need me at the sowing time, but you are my sister, and one cannot disown one's flesh and blood."

"We shall see now," resumed Frau von Bleichroden, "whether this air and this new treatment will help towards his cure. What do you think?"

"Certainly it will," her brother answered, but turned his head aside so that she should not see the doubt in his face.

"What a winter I have passed through in Frankfort! To think that Destiny can invent such tragedies! I think I could have borne his death more easily than this living burial."

"But one must always hope," said her brother in a hopeless tone. And his thoughts travelled far—to his children and his fields. But immediately afterwards he felt ashamed of his selfishness, that he could not sympathise fully with this grief, which was really not his own but which he had to share, and he felt angry with himself.

Suddenly there sounded from the hill above a shrill, prolonged scream, like the whistle of a locomotive, and then another.

"Does the train go so high up the mountain?" asked Frau von Bleichroden.

"Yes, it must be that," said her brother, and listened with wide-open eyes.

The scream was repeated. But now it sounded as if someone were drowning.

"Let us go home again," said Herr Schantz, who had become quite pale; "you cannot climb this hill to-day, and to-morrow we will be wiser and take a carriage."

But his sister insisted on proceeding in spite of all. And so they ascended the long hill to the hospital, though it was like a climb up Calvary. Through the green hawthorn hedges on both sides of the way, darted black thrushes with yellow beaks; grey lizards raced over the ivy-grown walls and disappeared in the crevices. It was full spring, for there had been no winter, and by the edges of the path bloomed primroses and hellebores; but they did not arrest the attention of the pilgrims. When they had got half-way up the hill, the mysterious screaming was repeated. As though overcome by a sudden foreboding, Frau von Bleichroden turned to her brother, looked in his eyes with her own, which were clouding over, only to see her fears confirmed, then she sank down on the path without being able to utter a cry, while a yellow cloud of dust whirled over her. And there she remained lying.

Before her brother could collect himself a casual passer-by had run for a carriage, and as the young woman was carried into it her work for the coming generation had already begun, and now two cries were heard—the cries of two human creatures from the depths of sorrow.

Her brother stood on the pathway looking up to the blue sky of spring, and thought to himself, "If the cries could only be heard up there, but it is certainly too high."

In the hospital which stood above them, Von Bleichroden had been lodged in a room which had an open view towards the south. The walls were padded and painted with flowing contours of landscapes in faint blue. On the ceiling was painted an espalier with vine leaves. The floor was carpeted, and under the carpet was a layer of straw. The furniture was completely covered with horsehair and cushions, so that no corners or edges of the wood were visible.

The situation of the door could not be discovered from within the room, thereby diverting all the patient's thoughts of getting out and the consciousness of being confined, the most dangerous of all to a mind in a state of excitement. The windows, it is true, were grated, but the gratings were elaborately wrought in the shape of lilies and leaves, and so painted that their purpose was quite disguised.

Von Bleichroden's madness had taken the form of torments of conscience. He imagined that he had murdered the keeper of a vineyard under mysterious circumstances, which he could never bring himself to confess for the simple reason that he could not remember them. Now he thought himself condemned to death and sitting in prison awaiting the execution of the sentence. But he had lucid intervals. Then he fastened large sheets of paper on the walls of the room and wrote syllogisms on them till they were covered. Then he remembered that he had caused some franc-tireurs to be shot, but did not remember that he was married. When his wife came to see him he received her visit like that of a pupil to whom he was giving lessons in logic. He had written up as the premise of his syllogisms, "All franc-tireurs are traitors and the order is to shoot them." One day his wife, who was obliged to agree with everything, had the rashness to shake his belief in the premise that "all franc-tireurs are traitors," thereupon he tore down all the syllogisms from the wall and said that he would spend twenty years in proving the premise, for premises must first be proved.

Besides this, he cherished great projects for the good of mankind. What is the object of all our striving here upon earth? he asked. Why does the king reign, the priest preach, the poet write, the artist paint? In order to procure nitrogen for the body. Nitrogen is the dearest of all kinds of food, and that is why meat is so expensive. Nitrogen is intelligence, for the rich who eat meat are more intelligent than the others who only eat vegetable hydrates. Now (so ran his argument) nitrogen was beginning to be scarce on the earth and this was why there came wars, workmen's strikes, newspapers, pietists and *coups d'état*. Therefore it was necessary to discover a new nitrogen mine. Von Bleichroden had done so, and now all men would be equal; liberty, equality and fraternity would arrive and be realised on earth. This inexhaustible mine was—the air. It contained seventy-nine per cent of nitrogen, and a means must be devised of inhaling it directly and of using it for the nourishment of the body without the necessity of it being first condensed into grass, corn and vegetables, and then converted by an animal into flesh. That was the problem of the future with which Von Bleichroden was busying himself; its solution would render agriculture and cattle-breeding superfluous, and the golden age would return on earth. But at intervals he again sank into dreams about the murder he supposed himself to have committed, and was profoundly miserable.

The same February morning on which his wife had been on her way to the asylum and had been obliged to return, Von Bleichroden sat in his new room and looked out of the window. At first he had contemplated the vine painted on the ceiling and the landscape on the walls; then he set himself in a comfortable chair opposite the window so that he had a clear view in front of him. He felt quiet to-day, for he had taken a cold bath the evening before and had slept well. He knew that the month was February, but he did not know where he was. The first thing that struck him was the absence of snow out of doors, and that surprised him for he had never been in southern lands. Outside in front of the window stood green bushes—the "laurier teint" quite covered with flowers, the "laurier cerise" with its shining bright green leaves, green through the whole winter. There was also a box tree and an elm quite overgrown with ivy which concealed all the branches and gave the tree the appearance of being in full leaf. Over the lawn, which was starred with primroses, as though a shower of sulphur had fallen on it, a man passed mowing the grass with a scythe, while a little girl was raking the beds.

Von Bleichroden took an almanac and read "February." "Raking in February! Where am I?" he asked himself. Then his eyes travelled beyond the garden and he saw a deep valley which sank gradually but was as green as a summer meadow. Little villages and churches stood here and there, and he could see bright green weeping-willows. "In February!" he said to himself again. And where the meadows ceased there lay a lake, quite calm and clear blue as air. On the other side of the lake was a landscape fading in azure tints, topped by a chain of hills. But above the chain of hills were some other objects which resembled clouds. They were of as delicate a white as fresh-washed wool, but they were pointed and over them lay small thin clouds. He did not know where he was, but it was so beautiful that it could not be on the earth. Was he dead, and had he entered another world? He was certainly not in Europe. Perhaps he was dead! He sank into quiet musing and sought to realise his new situation.

But when he looked up again he saw that the whole sunny picture was framed and crossed by the window-grating; the hammered iron lilies and the leaf-work stood out in sharp relief as though they were floating in the air. He was at first startled, but then he composed himself; he contemplated the picture once more, especially the pointed rosy clouds (as he thought them). Then he felt a wonderful joy and sensation of relief in his head: it was as though the convolutions of his brain, after having been hopelessly entangled, began to arrange and order themselves. He was so glad that he began to sing, as he thought, but he had never sung in his life and therefore he only uttered cries of joy. It was these which had issued from the window and filled his wife with grief and despair. After sitting thus for an hour, he had remembered an old painting in a bowling alley near Berlin which represented a Swiss landscape, and now he knew that he was in Switzerland and that the pointed clouds were Alps.

When the doctor made his second round he found Von Bleichroden sitting quietly in a chair before the window and humming to himself, and it was not possible to divert his gaze from the beautiful scene. But he was quite clear in his mind and fully realised his situation.

"Doctor," he said, pointing to the grated window, "why do you want to spoil and fleur-de-lisify such a beautiful picture? Won't you let me go into the open air? I think it would do me good, and I promise not to run away."

The doctor took his hand in order to feel his pulse secretly with his forefinger.

"My pulse is only seventy, doctor," said the patient, smiling, "and I slept well last night. You have nothing to fear."

"I am glad," said the doctor, "that the treatment has really had some effect on you. You can go out."

"Do you know, doctor," said the patient with an energetic gesture, "do you know that I feel as though I had been dead and come to life in another planet—so beautiful does it all seem. Never did I dream that the earth could be so wonderful."

"Yes, sir, the earth is still beautiful where civilisation has not spoilt it, and here nature is so strong that it resists the efforts of men. Do you think that your own country was always so ugly as it now is? No; where now there are waste sandy plains, which could not nourish a goat, there formerly rustled noble woods of oak, beech and fir, under whose shadow beasts of the chase fed, and where fat herds of the Norse-men's best kine fattened themselves on acorns."

"You are a disciple of Rousseau, doctor," broke in the patient.

"Rousseau was a Genevese, sir. There on the margin of the lake, deep in the bay which you see above the top of the elms, he was born and suffered, and there his 'Emile' and 'Contrat Sociale,' the gospels of nature, were burnt. There on the left, at the foot of the Valais Alps, in little Clarens, he wrote the book of love, 'La Nouvelle Heloise,' for it is the Lake of Geneva which you see."

"The Lake of Geneva!" repeated Von Bleichroden.

"In this quiet valley," continued the doctor, "where peaceful men live, many wounded spirits have sought healing. See there to the right, immediately above the little promontory with the tower and the poplars, lies Ferney. Thither fled Voltaire when he had finished his rôle of 'persifleur' in Paris, and there he cultivated the ground and erected a temple to the Supreme Being. Farther on lies Coppet, where lived Madame de Staël, the worst enemy of Napoleon, the betrayer of the people, who dared to teach the French, her countrymen, that the German nation was not France's barbarian enemy, for nations do not hate each other. Look now to the left; hither to this quiet lake fled the shattered Byron who, like a bound Titan, had torn himself loose from the trammels by which a period of reaction had endeavoured to imprison his strong soul, and here below he wrote the 'Prisoner of Chillon,' to express his intense hatred of tyrants. There under the lofty Mount Grammont he was nearly drowned one day before the little fishing village St Gingolphe, but his life was not yet finished. Hither fled all who could not tolerate the infected air which spread like a cholera over Europe after the conspiracy of the Holy Alliance against the newly won rights of the Revolution, that is, of mankind. Here, a thousand feet below you, Mendelssohn composed his melancholy songs, and Gounod wrote his 'Faust.' Can you not see whence he derived his inspiration for the 'Witches' Night,'—there, in the precipices of the Savoy Alps? Here Victor Hugo composed his fierce satires against the treachery of Napoleon III.; and here (strange irony of fate!) below in little quiet retired Vevey, where the north wind can never come, your own Kaiser sought to forget the terrible scenes of Sadowa and Königgratz. There the Russian Gortschakoff hid himself when he felt the ground shaking beneath his feet; here Lord Russell washed off the dust of politics and breathed pure unpolluted air; here Thiers sought to reduce to order his inconsistent, but, as I believe, honest schemes, often confused by political storms, and may he now, when he is to support the destinies of his people, remember the innocent hours in which his spirit communed with itself before the mild but solemn majesty of nature! And look over to Geneva, sir! There dwells no king with his court, but there was born a thought which is as great as Christianity, and whose apostles also carry a cross, a red cross on their white flags. When the Mauser rifles shot at the French eagle and the Chassepot at the German eagle, the red cross was held sacred by those who did not bow before the black cross, and in this sign, I believe, the future will conquer."

The patient, who had listened quietly to this strange speech which was as emotional, not to say sentimental, as if it had come from a preacher instead of a doctor, felt bored. "You are an enthusiast, doctor," he said.

"So will you be when you have lived here three months," answered the physician.

"You believe then in the treatment?" asked the patient somewhat less sceptically than before.

"I believe in the inexhaustible power of nature to heal the sickness of civilisation," he answered. "Do you feel strong enough to hear a good piece of news?" he continued, watching his patient closely.

"Quite, doctor!"

"Well then, peace has been made!"

"God! What a happiness!" the patient burst out.

"Yes certainly," said the doctor; "but don't ask more, for you cannot hear more to-day. Come out now, but be prepared for one thing. Your recovery will not be so rapid as you think. You may have relapses. Memory, you see, is our worst enemy,—but come with me now."

The doctor took his patient's arm and led him into the garden. There were no railings and no walls to bar one's passage, but only green hedges, which conducted the wanderer back by labyrinthine paths to his starting-point; but behind the hedges were deep trenches which were impossible to cross.

The lieutenant sought for familiar phrases with which to express his delight, but he felt that they were so inadequate that he resolved to be silent, listening to a wonderful soundless nerve music. He felt as though all the strings of his soul were being tuned again, and he experienced a calm such as he had not felt for a very long time.

"Do you doubt whether I am recovered?" he asked the doctor with a melancholy smile.

"You are on the way to recovery, as I told you before, but you are not quite well."

They found themselves now before a little arched stone door through which patients, accompanied by keepers, were passing.

"Where are all these men going?" asked the lieutenant.

"Follow them and you will see," said the doctor. "You have my permission."

Von Bleichroden entered, but the doctor beckoned to a keeper. "Go down to the Hôtel Faucon to Frau von Bleichroden," he said. "Give her my respects, and say that her husband is on the way to recovery but has not yet asked after his wife. When he does that he is saved."

The keeper went, and the doctor followed his patient through the little stone gate.

Von Bleichroden had entered a large hall which resembled no room that he had even seen before. It was neither a church, nor a theatre, nor a school, nor a town hall, but a little of all together. At the end of it was an apse which opened in three windows filled with painted glass. The colours harmonised with each other as though composed by a great artist's hand, and the light which entered was resolved, as it were, into one great harmonic major chord. It made the same impression on the patient as the C Major chord with which Haydn disperses the darkness of chaos, when at the creation the Lord, after the choir have been long painfully toiling at disentangling the disordered forces of nature, suddenly calls out "Let there be light!" and cherubim and seraphim join in.

Under the window was a rock of stalactite formation, shaped like an arch, from which trickled a little stream falling into a basin overhung by two arum lilies whose cups were as white as angels' wings. The pillars which enclosed the apse were constructed in no familiar architectural style, and their shafts were covered up to the roof with soft brown liver-wort. The lower panelling of the wall was covered with fir twigs, and the walls themselves were decorated by leaves of ever-green plants—laurel, holm-oak and mistletoe—arranged in designs of no particular style. Sometimes they seemed about to form letters, but lost themselves in faint fantastic flourishes, like Raphael's arabesques. Under the window apertures hung large wreaths as if for a May festival, and along the frieze of the ceiling there ran a design which had nothing in common with the lotus borders of Egypt, the meandering curves of Greece, the Acanthus decorations of Rome, or the trefoil and crucifers of the Gothic style.

Von Bleichroden looked about him and found the place provided with benches where the patients of the institute sat absorbed in silent wonder. He took a seat on one of them and heard someone sighing near him. Then he perceived a man about forty years old who had covered his face with his hands and wept. He had an aquiline nose, moustache and pointed beard, and his profile resembled those which Von Bleichroden had seen on French coins. He was certainly a Frenchman. Here then they were to meet, enemy with enemy, both somewhat tearful! Why? Because they had fulfilled their duties towards their respective fatherlands! Herr von Bleichroden felt excited and uneasy when he suddenly heard a strain of faint music. The organ was playing a chorale, but a chorale in the major key; it was neither Lutheran, nor Catholic, nor Calvinist, nor Greek, yet it spoke a language, and the patient thought he heard hopeful and comforting words. Then a man got up by the apsis and stood there half hidden by the stalactite rock. Was he a priest? No, he was dressed in a light grey coat, wore a bright blue cravat, and displayed an open shirt-front. He had no book with him, but spoke gently and simply as one speaks among friends. He spoke of the simple teaching of Christianity—to love one's neighbour as oneself; to be patient, tolerant, and forgiving towards enemies. He recalled how Christ had conceived of humanity as one, but how the evil nature of man had counteracted this great idea—how men had grouped themselves into nations, sects and schools; but he also expressed his firm hope that the principles of Christianity would soon be realised. He came down after speaking for a quarter of an hour, and offering a short prayer to God the Omnipotent without introducing any names which might remind his hearers of a formal creed or rouse their passions.

Herr von Bleichroden awoke as though from a dream. He had, then, been in church—he who, weary of all petty religious strifes, had not been to a service for fifteen years! And here, in a lunatic asylum, it was his fortune to find a Free Church fully realised. Here sat Roman Catholics, Greek Catholics, Lutherans, Calvinists, Zwinglians, Anglicans side by side and worshipped the same God in common. What a crushing criticism this church hall suggested for all those sects, born of the selfishness of men, which massacred, burnt and despised each other! What a handle did it supply for the attack of the "heretical" church on this political and dynastic Christianity!

Herr von Bleichroden let his gaze wander over the beautiful hall in order to drive away the terrible pictures which his imagination had conjured up. His eye roamed about till it fastened on the wall opposite the apse. There hung a colossal wreath, in the centre of which stood a word whose letters were formed of fir twigs. It was the French word "Noel," followed by the German "Weihnacht." What poet had arranged this hall? What knower of men, what deep mind had so understood how to awaken the most beautiful and purest of all recollections? Would not an overclouded mind feel an eager longing for light and clearness when it recollected the festival of light commemorating the end or, at any rate, the beginning of the end of the dark days at the turn of the year? Would not the recollection of childhood, when no religious strifes, no political hatred, no ambitious empty dreams had obscured the sense of right in a pure conscience—would it not stir a music in the soul louder than all those wild-beast bowlings which one had heard in life in the struggle for bread, or more often for honour?

He continued to meditate, and asked himself, how is it that man, so innocent as a child, afterwards becomes so evil as he grows older? Is it education and school, these lauded products of civilisation, which teach us to be bad? What do our first school-books teach us? They teach us that God is an Avenger Who punishes the sins of the fathers in the children unto the third and fourth generation; they teach us that those men are heroes who have roused nation against nation, and pillaged lands and kingdoms; that those are great men who have succeeded in obtaining honour the emptiness of which all see, but after which all strive; and that true statesmen are those who accomplish great and not high aims in a crafty manner, whose whole merit consists in want of conscience, and who will always conquer in the struggle against those who possess one. And in order that our children may learn all this, parents make sacrifices and renunciation and suffer the great pain of separation from their offspring. Surely the whole world must be a lunatic asylum, if this place was the most reasonable one he had ever been in!

Now he looked again at the only written word in the whole church, and spelt it over again; then there began to rise in the secret recesses of his memory a picture, as when a photographer washes a grey negative plate with ferrous sulphate as soon as he has taken it out of the camera. He thought he saw his last Christmas Eve represented before him. The last? No! Then he was in Frankfort. Then it was the last but one. It was the first evening he had spent in his fiancée's house, for they had been betrothed the day before. Now he saw the home of the old pastor, his father-in-law; he saw the low room with the white sideboard, the piano, the chaffinch in the cage, the balsam plants in the window, the cupboard with the silver jug on it, the tobacco pipes—some of meerschaum, some of red clay—and the daughter of the house going about hanging nuts and apples on the Christmas tree. The daughter of the house! It was like a flash of lightning in the darkness, but of beautiful, harmless summer lightning which one watches from a veranda without any fear of being struck. He was betrothed, he was married, he had a wife—his own wife who reunited him to life which he had previously despised and hated. But where was she? He must see and meet her now, at once! He must fly to her, otherwise he would die of impatience.

He hastened out of the church, and immediately met the doctor who had been waiting for him to see the effect of his visit to it. Herr von Bleichroden seized him by the shoulders, looked him straight in the eyes, and said with a kind of gasp, "Where is my wife? Take me to her at once. At once! Where is she?"

"She and your daughter," said the doctor quietly, "are waiting for you below in the Rue de Bourg."

"My daughter! I have a daughter!" interrupted the patient, and began weeping.

"You are very emotional, Herr von Bleichroden," said the doctor, smiling.

"Yes, doctor, one must be so here."

"Well, come and dress for going out," answered the doctor, and took his arm. "In half an hour you will be with your family and then you will be with yourself again." And they disappeared into the front hall of the institute.

Herr von Bleichroden was a completely modern type. Great grandson of the French Revolution, grandson of the Holy Alliance, son of the year 1830, like an ill-starred sailor he had made shipwreck between the cliffs of revolution and reaction. When between twenty and thirty years of age his intellect awoke and he realised in what a tissue of lies, both religious and political, he was involved, he felt as though he were really awake for the first time, or as though he were the only sane man shut up in a mad-house. And when he could not discover a single aperture in the enclosing wall by which he might escape without being confronted by a bayonet or the muzzle of a gun, he fell into a state of despair. He ceased to believe in anything, even in the possibility of deliverance, and betook himself to the opium dens of pessimism, in order at any rate to benumb his pain since there was no cure. Schopenhauer became his friend and later on he found in Hartmann the most brutal teller of truth which the world has seen.

But society summoned him and demanded that he should enrol himself somewhere in its ranks. Von Bleichroden plunged into scientific study and chose one of the sciences which has the least to do with the present—geology, or rather that branch of it, palaeontology, which had to do with the animal and plant life of a past world. When he asked himself, "Is this of any use to mankind?" he could only answer, "It is useful solely to myself, as a kind of opiate." He could never read a newspaper without feeling fanaticism rising up in him like incipient madness, and therefore he held everything which could remind him of his contemporaries and the present at arm's length. He began to hope that he would be able to spend his days in a dearly earned state of mental torpor, quietly and with his sanity preserved.

Then he married. He could not escape nature's inexorable law regarding the preservation of the species. In his wife he had sought to regain all those inner elements which he had succeeded in eliminating from himself, and she became his old emotional "ego," over which he rejoiced quietly without quitting his entrenchments. In her he found his complement, and he began to collect himself; but he felt also that his whole future life was based upon two corner-stones. One was his wife; if she gave way, he and his whole edifice would collapse. When only two months after their marriage he was torn from her side, he was no longer himself. He felt as though he had lost one eye, one lung and one arm, and therefore also he fell so quickly asunder when the blow struck him.

At the sight of his daughter, a new element seemed to be introduced into what Von Bleichroden called his "natural soul" as distinguished from his "society soul," which was the product of education. He felt now that he was incorporated in the family, and that when he died he would not really die, but that his soul would continue to live in his child; he realised, in a word, that his soul was really immortal, even though his body perished in the strife between chemical elements. He felt himself all at once bound to live and to hope, though sometimes he was seized with despair when he heard his fellow-countrymen, in the natural intoxication of victory, ascribe the successful issue of the war to certain individuals, who, seated in their carriages, had contemplated the battle-field through their field-glasses. But then his pessimism seemed to him culpable, because he was hindering the development of the new epoch by a bad example, and he became an optimist from a sense of duty. He did not, however, venture to return home from fear of falling into despondency, but asked for his discharge, realised his small property, and settled down in Switzerland.

It was a fine warm autumn evening in Vevey in the year 1872. The clock in the little pension Le Cedre had given the signal for dinner by striking seven. Round the large dinner-table were assembled the inmates of the pension, who were all mutually acquainted and lived on terms of intimacy, as those do who meet in a neutral country.

Herr von Bleichroden and his wife had as their companions at the table the melancholy Frenchman whom we have already seen in the hospital church, an English, two Russians, a German and his wife, a Spanish family, and two Tyrolese ladies.

Conversation proceeded as usual, quietly and peacefully—sometimes falling into an almost emotional tone, at others touching on the most burning questions of the day, without however kindling a conflagration.

"Never did I believe that the earth could be so supernaturally beautiful as here," said Herr von Bleichroden, entranced with the view through the open veranda doors.

"Nature is beautiful elsewhere also," said the German, "but I believe our eyes were not healthy."

"That is true," answered the Englishman; "but it really is more beautiful here than anywhere else. Have you never heard, gentlemen, how the barbarians felt (they were Alemanni or Hungarians, I think) when they emerged on the Dent Jaman and looked down on the Lake of Geneva? They thought that the sky had fallen down on the earth, and were so alarmed that they turned back again. The guide-book says so positively."

"I believe," said one of the Russians, "that it is the pure air, free from falsehood, which one breathes here which causes us to find everything so beautiful, although I will not deny that the beauties of nature have a reflex action upon our minds and prevent them being entangled in all our old prejudices. But only wait; when the heirs of the Holy Alliance are dead, when the highest trees have been truncated, our little plants also will flourish in clear sunshine."

"You are right," said Herr von Bleichroden; "but we shall not need to truncate the trees. There are other, more humane ways of proceeding. There was once an author who had written a mediocre play the success of which depended on the way in which the principal female part was acted. He went to a *prima donna* and asked if she would undertake the rôle. She gave an evasive reply. Then he forgot himself so far as to remind her that, according to the rules of the theatre, she could be compelled to play the part. 'That is true,' she answered, 'but I can make difficulties.' We can also circumvent our chief opposing falsities. In England it is simply an affair of the budget. Parliament cuts down the grant to royal personages, and they go their way. That is the method of legal reform. Is it not, Mr Englishman?"

"Certainly!" answered the Englishman. "Our Queen has the right to play croquet and tennis, but she cannot meddle in politics."

"But the wars—the wars—will they never stop?" objected the Spaniard.

"When women get the vote, armies will be reduced," said Herr von Bleichroden. "Isn't it so, wife?"

His wife nodded assentingly.

"For," continued he, "what mother will permit her son, what wife her husband, what sister her brother to go into these battles? And when there is no one to excite men against one another, then the so-called race-hatred will disappear. 'Man is good but men are bad' said our friend Jean Jacques, and he was right. Why are men more peaceful here in this beautiful country? Why do they look more contented than elsewhere? Because they have not daily and hourly these schoolmasters over them; they know that they themselves have settled who is to rule them; above all things they have so little to envy and so little to annoy them. No royal retinues, no military parades, no pompous spectacles which tempt a weak man to admire what is ostentatious but false. Switzerland is the little miniature model after which the Europe of the future will be built up."

"You are an optimist, sir," said the Spaniard.

"Yes," answered Von Bleichroden; "formerly a pessimist."

"You believe then," continued the Spaniard, "that what is possible in a little country like Switzerland, with three million inhabitants and only three languages, is possible also for the whole of Europe?"

Von Bleichroden seemed to hesitate, when one of the Tyrolese spoke. "Pardon me," she said to the Spaniard, "you doubt whether this is possible for Europe with its six or seven languages. It is too bold an experiment, you think, to answer with so many nationalities. But suppose I were to show you a land with twenty nationalities, Chinese, Japanese, Negroes, and representatives of all the nations of Europe mingled—that would be the international kingdom of the future. Well! I have seen it for I have been in—America."

"Bravo!" said the Englishman. "Our Spanish friend is defeated."

"And you, sir," continued the Tyrolese, turning to the Frenchman, "you mourn over Alsace-Lorraine, I see! You regard a war of *revanche* as unavoidable, for you do not believe that Alsace-Lorraine can continue to remain German—you think the problem is insoluble."

The Frenchman sighed by way of assent.

"Well, when Europe is one confederation of states, as Herr von Bleichroden calls Switzerland, then Alsace-Lorraine will be neither French nor German but just simply Alsace-Lorraine. Is the problem solved?"

The Frenchman lifted his glass politely and thanked her, bowing his head with a melancholy smile.

"You smile," the courageous maiden resumed. "We have smiled all too long, the smile of despair and scepticism; let us cease doing so! You see most of the countries of Europe represented among us here. Among ourselves, where no cynic hears us, we can utter the thoughts of our hearts, but in parliament, in newspapers, and in books—there we are cowardly, there we dare not expose ourselves to ridicule, and so we swim with the stream. What, after all, is the use of being cynical? Cynicism is the weapon of cowardice. One is anxious about one's heart. Yes, it is disgusting to see one's entrails exposed at a shop door, but to see those of others lying on the battle-field, while music and a rain of flowers await the returning conquerors—that is splendid! Voltaire was cynical, because he was still anxious about his heart, while Rousseau vivisected himself, tore his heart out of his breast, and held it against the sun, as the old Aztec priests did when they sacrificed—yes, there was method in their madness. And who has changed human kind—who told us that we were all wrong? Rousseau! Geneva yonder burnt his books, but modern Geneva has raised a memorial to him. What each of us here thinks privately, all think privately. Give us only freedom to say it aloud!"

The Russians raised their black tea-glasses and vociferated words in their language which only they understood. The Englishman filled his glass and was about to propose a toast, when the servant-maid came in and handed him a telegram. The conversation stopped for a moment; the Englishman read the telegram with visible emotion, folded it up, placed it in his pocket, and sank in thought. Herr von Bleichroden sat silent, absorbed in contemplation of the beautiful landscape outside. The Mont Grammont and the Dent d'Oche were lit up by the afterglow of the descended sun, which also dyed red the vineyards and chestnut-groves on the Savoy shore; the Alps glimmered in the damp evening air, and seemed as unsubstantial as the lights and shades; they stood there like disembodied powers of nature, dark and terrible on their reverse side, threatening and gloomy in their hollows, but on their sun-fronting sides, bright, smiling and joyful. Von Bleichroden thought of the concluding words of the Tyrolese, and fancied he saw in Mont Grammont a colossal heart with its apex looking towards the sky—the wounded, scarred, bleeding heart of humanity which turned itself towards the sun in a concentrated ardour of sacrifice, prepared to give all, its best and its dearest, in order to receive all. Then the dark, steel-blue evening sky was cut through by a streak of light, and above the low-lying Savoy shore there rose a rocket of enormous size. It rose high, apparently as high as the Dent d'Oche; it hung suspended as though it were looking round on the beautiful earth outspread beneath it before it burst. Thus it hesitated for a few seconds and then began the descent; but it had not gone many yards before it exploded with a report which took two minutes to reach Vevey. Then there spread out something like a white cloud which assumed a four-cornered rectangular shape, a flag of white fire; a moment after there was another report, and on the white flag appeared a red cross.

All the party sprang up and hastened into the veranda.

"What does that mean?" exclaimed Herr von Bleichroden, startled.

No one could or would answer, for now there rose a whole volley of rockets as if discharged from a crater over the peaks of the Voirons, and scattered a shower of fire which was reflected in the gigantic mirror of the lake.

"Ladies and gentlemen!" said the Englishman, raising his voice, while a waiter placed a tray with filled champagne glasses on the table. "Ladies and gentlemen!" he repeated, "this means, according to the telegram which I have just received, that the first International Tribunal at Geneva has finished its work; this means that a war between two nations, or what would have been worse—a war against the future, has been prevented; that a hundred thousand Americans and as many Englishmen have to thank this day that they are alive. The Alabama Question has been settled not to the advantage of America, but of justice, not to the injury of England, but for the good of future generations. Does our Spanish friend still believe that wars are unavoidable? When our French friend smiles again, let him smile with the heart and not with the lips only. And you, my German pessimist friend, do you believe now that the franc-tireur question can be settled without franc-tireurs and fusillades, but also only in this way? And you, Russian gentlemen, whom I do not know personally, do you think your modern method of forestry by truncating trees is the only correct one? Do you not think it is better to go to the roots? It is certainly a safer and quieter way. To-day, as an Englishman, I ought to feel depressed, but I feel proud on account of my country, as an Englishman always does, you know; but to-day I have a right to be so, for England is the first European Power which has appealed to the verdict of honourable men, instead of to blood and iron. And I wish you all many such defeats as we have had to-day, for that will teach us to be victorious. Raise your glasses, ladies and gentlemen, for the Red Cross, for in this sign we will certainly conquer."

Herr von Bleichroden remained in Switzerland. He could not tear himself away from this wonderful scenery which had led him into another world more beautiful than that which he had left behind.

Occasionally he had attacks of conscience, but this his doctor ascribed to a nervousness which is only too common among cultivated people at the present time. He resolved to elucidate the problem of conscience in a little pamphlet which he proposed to publish. He had read it to his friends and it contained some remarkable passages. With his German gift of penetration, he had reached the heart of the matter, and discovered that there are two kinds of conscience; first the natural, and second the artificial. The first conscience, he maintained, was the natural feeling of right. That was the conscience which had weighed on him so heavily when he had the franc-tireurs shot. He could only free himself from this by regarding himself persistently as a victim of the upper classes. The artificial conscience again originated in the power of habit and the authority of the upper classes. The power of habit rested so heavily on Herr von Bleichroden that sometimes when he went for a walk before noon he felt as though he had neglected his work in the Geological Bureau, and became uneasy and restless, like a boy who has played truant from school. He took incredible pains to exculpate himself by the consideration that he had obtained lawful leave of absence. But then he remembered vividly his room in the geological department, his colleagues who kept a keen watch on each other in order to discover a slip on another's part which might lead to their own advancement; and the heads of the department anxiously on the look-out for orders and distinction. He felt then as though he had absconded from it all.

Sometimes too he was attacked by the official conscience which the authority of the upper classes imposes on a man. He found it hard to obey the first commandment—to love one's King and fatherland. The King had plunged his fatherland into the misery of war in order to obtain a new fatherland for a relative, i.e. to make a Spaniard out of a Prussian.

Had the King shown love to his fatherland in this? Had kings, generally speaking, loved their fatherland? England was ruled by a Hanoverian, Russia was governed by a German Czar and would soon receive a Danish empress, Germany had an English Crown-princess, France a Spanish empress, Sweden a French king and a German queen.

If, following such high examples, people changed their nationality like a coat, Herr von Bleichroden believed that cosmopolitanism would have a brilliant future. But the commands of the authorities, which did not accord with their practice, worried him. He loved his country as a cat loves her warm place by the fire; but he did not love it as an institution. Sovereigns find nations necessary to provide them with conscript armies, as tax-payers and as supporters of the throne, for without nations there would not be any royal houses.

After Herr von Bleichroden had resided two and a half years in Switzerland, he received one day a summons from Berlin, for there were rumours of war in circulation. This time it was Prussia against Russia—the same Russia which three years previously had lent Prussia its "moral support" against France. He did not think it conscientious to march against his friends, and since he was quite sure that the two nations wished each other no ill, he asked his wife's advice what he should do in such a new dilemma, for he knew by experience that woman's conscience is nearer the natural law of right than man's.

After a moment's reflection, she answered "To be a German is more than to be a Prussian—that is why the German Confederation was formed; to be a European is more than to be a German; to be a man is more than to be a European. You cannot change your nation, for all 'nations' are enemies, and one does not go over to the enemy unless one is a monarch like Bernadotte or a field-marshal like Von Moltke. The only thing left is to neutralise yourself. Let us become Swiss. Switzerland is not a nation."

Herr von Bleichroden considered this such a happy and simple solution of the difficulty that he at once set about making inquiries how he could be neutralised. His surprise and delight can be imagined when he found that he had already fulfilled all the conditions required to become a Swiss citizen (for there are no underlings in that land!) as he had resided two years there.

Herr von Bleichroden is now neutralised, and although he is very happy he occasionally, though more seldom than before, has conflicts with his conscience.

OVER-REFINEMENT

Sten Ulffot, a youth of twenty years, the last scion of the ancient family of Ulffot, who possessed property in Wäringe, Hofsta and Löfsala, awoke one sunny May morning towards the end of the year 1460 in his bedroom at Hofsta in Upland. After some hours of dreamless sleep his rested brain began to review the events of the previous day, which had been of such decisive importance for him that, still benumbed by the blow, be stood as it were outside the whole affair and regarded it with wonder. The bailiff and sheriff's officer had been there, had shown mortgage-deeds of the house and estate, had read various parchment documents, and the upshot of it all was that Sten, because of his father's and his own debts, was reduced to abject poverty. And since his father in his lifetime had not been a merciful man, the young man must leave the old house, which was no longer his, the very next day.

Sten, who had never taken life seriously, for the simple reason that life had always been an easy matter for him, took this also very easily. Poverty for him was simply an uttered word which as yet lacked any corresponding reality. With a light heart he sprang out of bed, and put on his only but handsome velvet jacket and his only pair of breeches of Brabant cloth. He counted his few gold coins, and hid them carefully in his bosom, for he had now caught some idea of their importance. Then he went into the castle-room, which was quite empty.

The only impression this spacious room made on him was that he could breathe more easily in it. Upon a table fastened to the wall were to be seen damp rings—the traces left by the tankards of beer which the two functionaries had used the day before; it occurred to him that there would have been more rings if he had been with them himself—it looked so stingy!

The sun threw the reflections of the painted windows on the floor, so that they resembled beautiful mosaic work. His coat of arms, the wolf's foot on a red ground, was repeated six times; he amused himself by treading on the black foot, expecting to hear the wolf howl, but every time he did so the reflection of the wolf's foot merely lay on his yellow leather boots. When he took a step forward the reflection of the foot flew up to his breast and on his white jacket the red shield lay like a bleeding heart torn by the black paw with its outspread claws. He felt his heart beat violently and left the room.

He climbed the narrow stone stairs to the upper story, which his parents had occupied in their lifetime. There every possible movable which makes a house into a home for living beings had been swept off and carried away. The rooms looked like a series of burial chambers, hewn out of one rock, intended for souls without bodies and without corporeal needs. But signs of the life which had been there were still remaining. Two grey spots on the floor showed where a bed had stood; there were two dark lines where the table had been', and between them were marks and scratches left by boots; a dark, irregular stain on the white-washed wall showed where his father had been accustomed to rest his head when he raised it from his work which lay on the table. Some coals from the fire-place had fallen into the room and left dark spots on the floor like those on a panther-skin.

In his mother's room was a stone image of the Virgin and Child fixed to the wall; she regarded her Son with a look full of hope and without any foreboding that she held a future condemned prisoner upon her knees. Young Sten felt a vague depression and went on. Through a secret door he mounted up into the attic and went out upon the roof. Underneath him he saw the whole wide-stretching expanse of land which till lately he had called his own: these green fields which once formed the bottom of the sea, surrounded by small green hills once islands, but lately wore their verdure on his account—to support the poor who clothed him, brushed him, prepared his food, and tended his horses, his hounds, his falcons and his cattle. In the previous autumn he had stood here and watched them sow his corn; now others would come and cut and gather it in. A little while ago it was his to decide when the fishes in the streams should die, when the firs in the wood should be felled, and when the game should be shot. Even the birds in this huge space of air belonged to him, although they had flown hither from the realm of the Emperor of Austria.

He could not yet grasp the fact that he possessed nothing more of all this, for he had never missed anything and therefore did not know what possession was; he only felt a huge emptiness and thought that the landscape had a melancholy look. The swallows which had come that very day flew screaming about him and sought their old nests in the eaves; some found them, and others did not—the rains of autumn and snows of winter had destroyed their little clay dwellings so that they had fallen into the castle-moat.

But there was clay in the fields, water in the brooks and straw on every hillock; as long as they were homeless they could find shelter in every grove and under the thatch of every cottage. They hunted without hindrance in their airy hunting grounds; they paired and wedded in the blue spring weather which was full of the sweet scents of the newly sprung birches, the honey-perfumed catkins of the osiers, and all the invisible burgeonings of the spring. He went farther up on the roof and stood by the pole that supported the dog-vane. As he looked up to the white clouds of spring sailing by, it seemed to him as though he stood on the aerial ship of a fairy-tale and were sailing among the clouds, and when he looked down on the earth again it appeared like a collection of mole-hills, a mere rubbish-heap cast out of heaven. But he had a foreboding that he must go down and dig in the mole-hills in order to find a living; he felt that his feet stood firm upon the earth, although his glances wandered at will among the silver-gleaming clouds.

As he descended the narrow attic stairs it seemed to him as though an enormous gimlet were screwing him deeper and deeper into the earth. He entered the garden and looked at the apple trees in blossom. Who would pluck the fruits of these trees which he had cultivated and tended for years? He looked at the empty stable; all his horses were gone except a sorry nag, which he had never thought worth riding. He went into the dog-house and saw only ten empty leash-straps. Then his heart grew heavy, for he felt that he had been parted from the only living creatures who loved him. All others—friends, servants, farm-hands, tenants—had, as his poverty increased, gradually changed their demeanour, but these ten had always remained the same. He was astonished that he did not feel the blank so bitterly up there in the ancestral castle with its memories, for he forgot that *that* sense of loss had long been obliterated by his tears.

He went into the courtyard of the castle. There a sight met his eyes which made him realise his true situation. On a four-wheeled wagon, to which three pairs of oxen were yoked, lay a heap of furniture and household utensils; beneath all lay the great oak bedstead splendidly carved, mighty clothes and linen chests constructed like fortresses against thieves, his father's work-table, the family dining-table, the chairs from the sitting-room with fragments of torn-down, gaudy-coloured curtains, his mother's embroidery-frame, his grandfather's chair with the cushioned arms and the high back, and on the top of all his own cradle and the praying stool at which his mother had so often prayed for her little one. Beside them were bundles of lances, swords, and shields with which his forefathers had once acquired and defended these goods which he must now leave behind in order to go out into the world and earn his bread in the sweat of his brow. All these dead things which, when in their places, had formed parts of his own self lay there like corpses and up-torn trees showing their roots; it was an enormous funeral pile of memories, which he would have liked to set fire to.

Just then the gates grated on their hinges, the drawbridge was lowered, the driver cracked his whip over the first pair of oxen, the ropes and shafts of the cart creaked, and the heavily laden vehicle rattled away on the stone-paved courtyard. As it rolled over the planks of the wooden, bridge, there was a rumbling like the echo from a grave-vault.

"The last load?" called the driver to the gate-keeper.

"The last," came the answer from the vaulted gateway.

The word "last" made a deep impression on Sten, who felt himself to be the last of his race, but he could not indulge in further reflections, for a man whom he did not know stepped towards him holding the nag.

"The castle is to be shut up," he said.

"Why shut up?" asked Sten, merely to hear his own voice again.

"Because it is to be pulled down. The King does not wish to have so many castles in the land."

Sten laid hold of the reins and mounted the nag; he pressed it with his knees, and holding his head high, rode through the arched gateway. There he took out his purse and threw a piece of gold behind him, which the gate-keeper and the stable-man raced for.

When he had ridden over the drawbridge, he reined in his horse till the cart with its load had disappeared from sight. Then he turned up a narrow path and vanished among the birch trees.

"I wonder what he will do?" said the gate-keeper.

"Enlist," answered the stable-man.

"No, he is no good at that; he has learnt nothing but reading and writing."

"Then he will become one of the King's secretaries."

"Not *this* King's; his father was in disfavour for refusing to bear arms against his fellow-countrymen."

"Then let him become what the devil he likes."

"One cannot become what one likes, one must become what one can; and if one can do nothing, one becomes nothing."

"Just so it is! Just so! But I don't know what one has to learn in order to become a gate-keeper."

"Well, one must be strong enough for it, and keep awake at night; and that the young gentleman cannot do."

"Yes, he can keep awake at night, for we have seen him do it; but perhaps he is not strong enough to draw the heavy chain."

"Well, stable-man, he must look after himself. Meanwhile I will draw up the bridge, and then we can go the backway to the tavern, and change our piece of gold, and he can do what he likes!"

"What he can, gate-keeper; one cannot do what one likes."

"Quite true! Quite true!"

The chain rattled, the bridge was drawn up, and the gate fell to with a dull crash.

Sten meantime had ridden for several hours without exactly knowing whither. He only knew that the way led him out into the world, far from the protection of home. He saw by the sun's position that it was nearly afternoon, and by the nag's drooping head that it was tired; he therefore dismounted, tied the reins loosely round one of the horse's forelegs and led him up from the path to a fine upland meadow where he left him loose to graze. Then he lay down under a wild apple tree to rest, but since he felt that the ground was damp, he broke down some young birches and made a bed out of their soft leaves; he also tore off some long strips of bark and placed them under his head, knees and elbows; then he went to sleep. But when he awoke he felt terrible pangs of hunger, for he had eaten nothing during the last twenty-four hours; he felt his tongue cleaving to his palate and a burning and tickling feeling in his throat. The horse had disappeared. He did not know where he was, could not see a human habitation, and had small hope of finding an inn before nightfall. Then he fell on his knees and prayed his patron-saint to help him. As he mentioned the name "St Blasius" it occurred to him how the saint under similar circumstances had sustained himself on roots and berries in the desert. Strengthened by prayer, he looked round to see what there was to eat and drink. His eye first fell on a birch. It was just the time of year when the sap flows. With his knife he split off a piece of bark and fastened the corners together with wood splinters so that it formed a water-tight basket; then he bored a hole in the tree and from the hard wood trickled out the clear sap resembling Rhine wine in colour. While it was trickling, he climbed into the apple tree, where he had seen a large number of apples, which had hung there all the winter and were certainly rotten but could at any rate fill his stomach. When he had eaten some of them he began to shake the tree, so that the apples fell on the ground. He was just on the point of rejoicing at his discovery and looking forward to drink the good birch wine when he heard a harsh voice calling from below;

"Hullo, Sir thief! what are you doing there?"

"I am no thief," answered Sten.

"He who steals is a thief," answered the voice. "Come down at once, or you will spend the night in gaol."

Sten thought it belter to descend and try to explain himself. He found himself before a man of authoritative appearance, who was accompanied by a large dog.

"In the first place," said the man, "you have committed an outrage on a fruit-bearing tree; punishment—three marks and forfeiture of the axe—chapter seventeen of the forest laws."

"I thought one had a right to plunder wild trees," said Sten in a shamefaced way, for he had never been addressed in this manner.

"There are no wild trees now, though it was certainly so in Adam and Eve's time. Besides, I was purposely keeping the apples to flavour cabbages with. Secondly, you have cut and extracted the sap from my fine carriage-pole."

"Carriage-pole?"

"Yes, I intended to make a carriage-pole of the birch tree. Then you have peeled off birch bark in a wood that did not belong to you; fine —three shillings, according to the same chapter in King Christopher's land-law."

"I thought I was in God's free world and had a right to support my life," answered Sten mildly.

"God's free world? Where is that? I only know tax-free land, land that is assessed, and crown lands. Thirdly, probably—I have no testimony to that effect, but probably it is your horse which is feeding in my meadow?"

"It is my horse, and I suppose it could not die of hunger while the grass was growing round it."

"No one need die of hunger. Any animal can graze by the way-side, everyone can pluck a handful of nuts, and every traveller can cut an axle for his wheel when necessary. You are therefore convicted of fourfold robbery, and I keep the horse."

"And leave me alone in the wood, where perhaps I cannot even kindle a fire for the night."

"Whoever cuts dry wood on other people's land is liable to a fine of three shillings each time. If it were not so, one could never be sure of possessing anything."

"It never was so on my property. There we knew nothing of such laws and paragraphs, and my manorial rights were never so niggardly as yours."

Here a great alteration took place in the bearing of the man of authority. He took the horse by the rein, led it to Sten, held the stirrup for him, bent one of his knees, and said:

"Sir, pardon me, I see you have ridden out for recreation and jest with an old law-student. A few mouldy apples, I hope, will not make any trouble between us."

Sten, who was a lover of sincerity, hesitated a moment before putting his foot into the proffered stirrup, but as he was glad to be safely out of the difficulty, he swung himself up on his saddle.

"Listen," he said in an authoritative tone, "where is the nearest inn?"

"Half a mile southwards, if your lordship is going to Stockholm."

"Good! Now I thank you for the amusement, and put a small question to you. Tell me: if one steals out of necessity, then it is theft; and if one steals to amuse oneself, what is that?"

"A joke."

"Good. But how is the judge to know whether it is a joke or earnest?"

"Oh, he can tell!"

Sten pressed his nag's sides with his legs, bent forward, and said: "No, friend, he cannot."

The nag shot away like an arrow from the astonished law-student and his carriage-pole.

The prospect of soon obtaining a meal, and the fortunate conclusion of his adventure, had set Sten in a mood which banished gloomy reflections. After a half-hour's trot he rode through the gate of the inn, and was received like a gentleman of high rank. He sat down at a table under a great hawthorn tree outside the house, and ordered a fowl with sage stuffing and a jug of Travener beer. These the host promised to get even if he had to run round the whole village for them.

The May evening was fine, and Sten ate and drank at his ease, though he could not completely banish the alarm which the threatening attack of hunger had just caused him. He could not get the scene with the law-student out of his thoughts, and he felt that soon, when his fine velvet jacket no more protected him, he would come under the hard laws of necessity like any other ordinary man. He perceived that he must certainly become a working member of human society, and join one of its numerous classes if he wished to continue to live. The earth, with all the products that she bore, was already fully occupied, so that one of the lords of creation might lie on the ground and die of hunger under a fruit-bearing tree if he did not wish to be hung, while the birds of the air might eat their fill with impunity off the same tree. He wondered that men let squirrels and jays plunder hazel bushes, and preserve their freedom, while only in case of absolute need was a man allowed to save his life with a handful of nuts. It seemed to him a cruel contradiction; he might save his life, but not support it, and every meal was as it were a recurrent saving of life. But on the other hand his forefathers had founded these laws and he had himself employed them. Who then was the proper object of his reproach? Was not the fault partly his own, and were not the consequences quite natural?

While he was thus meditating, his eyes were fixed upon a figure which was approaching the garden of the inn from the highway. As it came nearer, Sten saw a man of about thirty with a dark complexion, long arms, and knees and feet curving inwards as though he were afflicted with spavin. Over his shoulder he carried a sack, and in his hand a knotted stick. With a jerk he flung the sack on the table close to Sten, sat down and struck on the table with the stick so sharply that it sounded like a pistol-shot. At the same time he called into the house, "Come out, Mr Innkeeper, and give a worthy member of the worshipful company of blacksmiths in Stockholm a jug of beer."

The innkeeper, who thought that some important person had come, hastened out, but when he saw the fellow he turned round and said to Sten in a disdainful tone: "These fellows never have money. I will give him nothing." "By St Michael, the archangel and St Loyus, innkeeper, if you don't give me beer I will set my mark upon you," broke in the man, and lifted his stick.

"If you threaten, you will be hung for compelling hospitality," said the innkeeper; "you did not pay the last time you were here, so pick up your sack and take yourself off, for the clerk of assize is sitting inside."

"I will pay for his beer, innkeeper," interrupted Sten, who felt a certain sympathy with the unmasked braggart.

"The gentleman is kind and understands a traveller's needs. As regards payment, I think it is all the same who pays. To-day it is my turn, to-morrow yours. In good company I never say 'no.' And a member of the worshipful company of blacksmiths at Stockholm can be as good a gentleman as any other, or any traveller, with your permission."

"You are right, sir; all things considered, we are all travellers, and when we travel we are all alike."

The blacksmith, who had received his jug of beer, lifted it, took his cap off, and said in a solemn voice, "Saint Michael and Saint Loyus!" Then he threw back his head and took some tremendously deep draughts of the beer, so that the muscles of his neck moved like the backs of snakes. Then he collected his breath, raised the jug once more and said, "Pledge me a toast, sir, with your permission." Then he drank for some minutes so that his neck sinews were strained like harness-straps. When he had finished, he emptied out the last drops, struck the table with his stick, and called into the house, "Two full jugs! Now I am the inviter."

"And the young gentleman pays?" asked the host.

Sten nodded assent, and the blacksmith continued, "It is all the same who pays. '*Commune bonum,*' as we say in the shop. To-day it is my turn, to-morrow yours."

"Sit down, sir, and let us talk," said Sten. "You are a blacksmith, I hear."

"Banner-bearer to the worshipful company of blacksmiths in Stockholm, thanks to St Michael and St Loyus, with your permission!"

"Tell me, is your trade hard?"

"Hard! Well, it is not for anyone. It is the hardest work there is. It is a trade which the world cannot dispense with. No one can get on without a blacksmith. Believe me when I say it. The Emperor of Rome had a councillor whose name was Vulcant and it was he who invented the blacksmith's art. And you ask if it is difficult!"

"Yes, but one could learn it," said Sten, who felt more amused than convinced.

"Learn it? No, sir, one cannot."

"But you have learnt it," insisted Sten.

"I! With me it is another matter," answered the blacksmith, contemplating the bottom of his mug.

"Well, why cannot it be another matter with me also?" objected Sten.

"Show me your fists, if you please, sir."

Sten laid two small white hands on the table.

The smith grinned. "They are no use. Look at mine." He took the pewter pot in a giant's grasp and squeezed it till it became as slender as an hour-glass.

Sten was still not convinced. "But you were not born with such fists," he said.

"Yes, sir, I was. I was born to be a blacksmith, just as you were born—to do nothing, if you will allow me to say so. What do you expect to do in the world with such mere pegs? You had better not depend on them or you will be disappointed."

"And yet I am thinking of becoming a blacksmith," said Sten innocently.

"You must not make a jest of that worshipful fraternity, sir. Besides, I should like to say that the times are different to what they were formerly; a blacksmith may become mayor or councillor, and Sir Vulcan, whom I mentioned just now, was one of the Emperor of Austria's councillors. One should not be proud, even if one is of high birth. King Karl Knutsson was King one day and the next day he was nothing. If he had learnt something, he would have been something."

"That is just what I wanted to say, dear smith. And I may as well say that I am not a gentleman though I have a velvet jacket."

"Is it a disguise? Aren't you a real gentleman?"

"I have been one, but now I am nothing."

The blacksmith drew up the corners of his mouth, came nearer, surveyed Sten and continued: "Come down in the world? What! Downhill? Eh! Hard times! When thieves fall out, honest folk come by their own. Yes, yes. No relations. No fine friends. Alone in the world. Obliged to work. And now you want to become a blacksmith, when you can't be anything else."

"If I can become one."

"No, you can become nothing. That is less than you are, Claus. (My name is Claus.) Now you can be proud, Claus. But I am not proud, and therefore I invite you again to the jug of beer to which I invited you just now. Was the fowl there good; it looks to me lean." Claus made a movement as though he were chewing something tough.

Sten answered: "The fowl was fat enough; will you have some?"

"If I can be quite sure that it is good; otherwise I don't care about it, for if I spend money I want to have something really good for it."

Sten ordered a fowl and fresh jugs of beer, and recommenced the conversation. "I hope you will recommend me to your guild or company."

"I will see what I can do, but one has to proceed warily with those gentlemen. Congratulate yourself that you have made acquaintance with the banner-bearer of the guild, for he is a powerful gentleman, although he goes round with a sack when he is on his journeys."

Sten, who was not accustomed to so much beer, at any rate of the sort which was served here, began to feel sleepy and rose up in order to go to his bedroom. But Claus could by no means He induced to agree to this.

"No, stay sitting, my dear," he said, "and drink a glass of wine with me. It is such a fine evening and you have not far to go to tied. If you get sleepy, I will carry you up the stairs."

But Sten could not possibly drink any more. Claus was annoyed and asked if he refused to drink with the guild's banner-bearer. Sten asked to be excused, but Claus would not consent. He said that Sten was proud, and should take care, for pride was always punished. Sten was so sleepy that he could hardly understand what was said, and clambered up the stairs to the attic where in the darkness he sought for a cushion, on which he fell asleep at once.

He had, as he thought, slept for quite twenty-four hours when he felt a burning sensation as though sparks of fire had fallen on his face. He sat up and found that the whole room was full of the hateful humming of a swarm of gnats which had gained admission. When he had somewhat shaken off his sleep, he could distinguish men's voices, and loudest among them the deep voice of his friend Claus.

"Oh, he is a devilish fine fellow. His father and I are very old friends. He has been a little spoilt by wearing fine clothes and so on, but we will soon drive it out of him. Innkeeper, more claret! Yes, you see his father was in my debt, and I waited. Take what you like, parish-clerk!"

Sten sprang up and saw through a chink in the wall how Claus sat at the end of the table and carried on a conversation with the innkeeper and a stranger, who was probably the parish-clerk. The table was covered with jugs and pots, and the party did not seem to have suffered from thirst.

The parish-clerk, who thought that the smith had talked long enough, now led the conversation. "Listen, Claus; you say that he is nothing, that he has no occupation and no money. Do you know what one calls such a gentleman?"

"No, no."

"Well, one calls him a tramp. And do you know what the law says about vagabond tramps?"

"No, no."

"It says that whoever chooses may take such a tramp by the collar and put him in gaol. And that is right, thoroughly right. God, you see, from the beginning, has created men to work, do service, and make themselves useful— —"

"Or to be rich," interrupted the innkeeper.

"Hush! Don't interrupt me—to make themselves useful in one way or another. Suppose," continued he, "that there are men who will not work; suppose that there are people who prefer to live at the expense of other people——"

Claus gave him a sharp look and seized his stick. But after taking a drink, the parish-clerk continued: "Then I ask—what is one to do with such people? Can anyone answer me?"

The innkeeper was about to answer, but the parish-clerk motioned him away with his left hand.

"Can anyone answer this? No, I say, for we know in part and prophesy in part. *Cur tuus benevolentium.*" He finished his mug and got up in order not to spoil the effect of his speech by a bad translation of the Latin.

Sten lay down again and put his head under his pillow. It seemed to him that he had slept another four-and-twenty hours when he was aroused by a foot pushing his bed very emphatically. He sat up and saw by the light of the dawn, which fell through a crevice in the wall, that his friend Claus, who apparently did not venture to stoop, stood on one foot, and laying hold of a beam was feeling in the bed with his foot for his sleeping friend. He accompanied this search with short exclamations—"You! you!" When he caught sight of Sten's face in the dim light he drew his foot back and said: "Do you know what you are, you? Do you know that you are a tramp? Do you know that you will be put into gaol if you do not eat someone else's bread, seeing you have none of your own. I tell you the sheriff is after you, and if you are not off by sunrise you will be imprisoned. Do you understand?"

Sten understood that there was a very good chance of it, as he had already overheard their talk; but he did not understand that one could not go one's own way to seek work, and Claus exerted himself in vain in order to explain to him that one must have work or be the possessor of such and such a sum. Sten, who feared imprisonment most of all, let himself be easily persuaded to take his horse out of the stable and to hand over some of his gold coins to Claus, who promised to settle with the innkeeper. The latter was quite willing, for he himself was liable to no less a punishment for having given lodging to a tramp. Sten shook the good blacksmith's hand, and promised to look him up in Stockholm.

Now he rode again on his horse, shaken out of his sleep, chased out of a casual lodging, flying from the danger of imprisonment, and firmly resolved to seek no other shelter till he reached the capital.

Two days later, on a Saturday afternoon, Sten reined in his horse on the top of the Brunkebergsasen ridge, on the side where it descends towards the Norrstrom River. Beneath him he saw for the first time the capital, the battle-field whereon struggles for power were waged. On these little rocky islands between the two water-courses, closely encircled by towers and walls, lived the population among whom he wished to enrol himself. The battle between King Karl Knutsson and Archbishop Jöns Bengtsson was at its height, but to Sten it was a matter of indifference who won, for his father had fallen into disfavour with the King, and his family had an old feud with the Archbishop. As the evening sun cast its horizontal rays on the flag which waved from the chief tower of the castle, he saw the arms of the Bondes—the boat against a white background—and knew how the land lay.

Although peace seemed to have been concluded for the time, the difficulty of entering the city gate was not less than before. He would in any case be obliged to give his name and to be registered, and perhaps have to say why he came and where he came from. In his tired mood he fancied he saw a thousand difficulties rise and the walls growing in height till they appeared insurmountable. He felt like a besieger who was thinking of a stratagem by means of which to enter the city. It was there he hoped to find the only place where he could earn his bread by means of the book-learning which he had acquired.

As he was sitting on the hill, lost in these serious meditations, he heard from the foot of it a sound of merry voices mingled with the music of trumpets and flutes. At the angle of the walls before the Klara Convent issued forth a gay stream of folk, disappearing and reappearing from behind the kitchen-gardens on the slope of the Bill. The procession drew nearer. At its head rode a youth, with a garland on his brow and a long spear-shaft wreathed with green in his hand. He was followed by pipers and trumpeters with gooseberry leaves in their caps; after him came a whole crowd of people with black cloth masks and red wooden masks, dressed in the most fantastic garb after Greek and Roman patterns; last of all, riding backwards on a sorry jade, a youth dressed in fur, with loosely streaming hair and beard, to represent winter. It was the procession of the "May-lord," greeting the advent of spring in the Klara district.

Sten seized the opportunity by the forelock, rode down the hill, and joined the procession. He passed through the gateway without being interfered with, although he thought he saw a pair of sharp eyes fastened on him under the archway itself. Meanwhile he could not help thinking how the guard's over-hasty inference "Cheerful people are not dangerous"—had been of use to him, who felt anything but cheerful. He felt easier in mind when he had passed through the gates of both the bridges.

The procession halted in the great market-place, where it broke up in order to reassemble in the restaurant of the town hall. This had received special permission to remain open all night, since the postponed May festival was being celebrated now because of the late spring and the King's victory.

Sten took up his quarters at an inn in the Dominicans' street, which bore an image of St Laurence painted on its signboard. When his horse had been placed in the stable he was shown up to the sleeping chamber. There he found a great number of beds without any chairs, and as the evening seemed too beautiful to remain indoors, he went out into the city in order to take a bath.

When he came out into the street again, he became somewhat depressed at seeing the narrow passages, called "streets," in which pale-faced people walked, breathing unwholesome air and treading in the dirt and kitchen offal thrown out of the doorways. The crowd kept streaming to and fro, and he wondered that they never came to an end nor seemed weary. The street itself, which was paved with rough cobbles, was difficult to walk on, and he did not understand why men should have gathered together these instruments of torture to make the way more stony than it naturally was. Of the sky there was only a grey strip to be seen between the rows of houses, and the high corbel-step gables rose like Jacob's-ladders, on which souls sought in vain to rise to the heights from their dark, evil-smelling dungeons.

He felt confused and astray. At one moment he was jostled by a porter, at another trod on by a horse; then he knocked his head against a window-board. All these people had crowded together on a little island and built on each other like bees in a honeycomb. Why? For mutual aid? He did not believe it.

After inquiring his way to the public baths in the Allmännings Gata, he felt a keen desire to free himself by a bath from the sensation of uncleanness which even the air he breathed oppressed him with. In the undressing-room which was shared by all, he found a great number of people of all classes, for it was Saturday evening. In the uncertain light he could not see them distinctly, but the pungent odour of perspiration exhaling from their bodies after severe physical labour, made him shudder. He undressed, put on bathing-drawers, and entered the bathroom.

In the midst of it stood an enormous walled fire-place in which a great fire was burning; round it, up to the roof, ran wooden galleries where men sat—some beating each other with rods, others drinking beer. Great stalwart women with tucked-up skirts poured jugs of water on the fire-place, which at once sent out clouds of steam. These the bathers allowed to envelop them, amid loud shrieks and laughter. One caught glimpses of naked bodies, matted beards and shining eyes. And what bodies! They seemed to Sten like a number of wild beasts with hairy breasts and limbs who did not need clothing, and those who, while they waited for their bath, danced before the fire reminded him of fairy-tales of distant lands where men walked with their heads under their arms and with one eye in their foreheads. He could not make up his mind to address any of them, though they were human beings like himself, but with a difference. They did not talk like him; they did not laugh like him; they were not shaped like him. The bones of their backs looked like the letter X, and their feet were turned inwards so that the toes met; nightwork and heat had rendered their faces emaciated. Was it through willing sacrifice for their fellow-men that they made themselves cripples, or were they compelled by necessity to do so? These smiths with shoulder-blades like knapsacks, with arms as long as the helve of a sledge-hammer, with the soles of their feet flattened and distorted; these tailors with thin chests, crooked legs as slender as sticks, and bent backs—were they conscious that their deformity set off the handsome appearance of others?

For a moment his aesthetic Sense was offended and he wished to go, but he was restrained by the thought that he must also soon perhaps undergo some similar deformity in order to perform his duty in this society into which he was now forced to enter as a retribution for his ancestors' mistake in withdrawing him from the lot which all were born to share. But the peasants, fishermen, and huntsmen he had formerly known, did not look like these! The former were like the trees of the wood, straight though knotted. Here in the working life of the town some mistake had been made, but he could not say what. He shyly approached one of the giantesses and asked if he could have a water bath.

The old woman looked at his white skin and his small hands and pushed him into a smaller room, where some empty bath-tubs stood on the ground.

"He is certainly a fine gentleman's son," she said, regarding him critically. "He has evidently come to the wrong place, but that does not matter." She laid the youth in the bath as though he were a child, and began to rub his skin with a horsehair brush.

"No! that will make holes in his skin, one can see. Yes, men are so different from each other. A foot like a girl's; one can see how the blood runs in the veins. I am sure that these fine folk have not the same blood as we. And such hands! Pure as those of St John which they have made of wax in Our Lady's chapel. They are not made to lay hold of with."

When the bath was ended, the old woman set Sten on a stool and dried him carefully, as though she were afraid of breaking one of his limbs. Then she took a comb and began to do his fair hair, talking to herself the while. "Pure silk and gold! One might weave a mass-robe for the Bishop from this hair!"

Then a gnat flew in through the window-opening and settled on Sten's bare shoulder; it had not long to look in order to find a place into which to sink its sting, for his skin was milk-white and soft after the warm bath.

The old woman stopped in her task, and observed almost with alarm how the uninvited parasite bled the fine gentleman; she saw how the gnat's transparent body filled itself with clear red blood, and how it lifted its front leg as if to seize its prey firmly. Then the giantess seized with the tips of her nails the little blood-letter by its wings and held it against the light.

"What is that?" asked Sten, and made a movement.

The old woman was too deep in her contemplation to answer at once. At last she said, "Ob, it was a gnat!"

"Which has got noble blood in its vein," broke in Sten. "Now do you think, old woman, that it is better than the other gnats?"

"That one cannot exactly know," said the giantess, still examining her captive. "Blood is thicker than water. I have seen many gnats in my time, but this one is something unusual. I should like to let it live."

"And to see how it would give itself airs over the other gnats. You would like to see it propagate young lord and lady gnats who would sit on silk and let themselves be fed by others. No, you shall see that it is just as plebeian as all the others, and that it has the same blood as you and can die as easily as its companion gnats outside."

He struck the old woman's finger with his hand, and there appeared only a bright red spot of blood upon it.

"Now was it not as I said?" she exclaimed. "It is as bright as red gold."

"That is because it is thinner," said Sten, "therefore it will soon be like pure water; and therefore you see the nobles will die and the serfs will live."

The conversation was over and Sten rose up, thanked his attendant, and went into the great bathroom where the noise was deafening owing to the beer and the heat combined. He hastened by the bathers into the undressing-room, where he found his clothes with difficulty under piles of leather trousers, smocks, and vests.

When he came out into the street he directed his steps through the Merchants' Gate to the Great Market. There he saw the town hall lit up; the great door which led to the underground restaurant was decorated with fir branches, weapons and flags. He descended the broad staircase, attracted by the music of violins, flutes, and trumpets. Although he did not think it reasonable that men should collect to enjoy themselves underground, when the earth itself was so spacious and beautiful, yet he felt bound to confess that the restaurant of the town hall presented an imposing appearance with its huge pillars which this evening were decked with garlands of fir twigs and bunches of liver-wort, anemones and cowslips. Enormous beer and wine barrels, arranged in rows, formed three great alleys running from the tap-room, which was adorned by a huge figure of Bacchus riding on a cask. In tubs filled with sand stood young firs and junipers, and the ground was strewn with cut fir twigs. The musicians sat on a gigantic barrel, and from the vaulted roof hung barrel-hoops with oil-lamps and wax-lights. An enormous number of people, half in disguise, half in their holiday clothes, stood in groups round the tables or walked down the tub-lined alleys. The joy seemed universal and genuine, for it had a natural cause—the arrival of spring, and a less natural one—the return of the King for the third time.

Sten wandered lonely among the festive groups, without the hope of meeting a friend. He felt thirsty after his bath but was ashamed to ask for anything, for he did want to drink alone. But as he walked he grew suddenly conscious that someone was looking at him. He turned round and saw a little yellow, dried-up, narrow-chested man who for want of a table had sat down by an upturned barrel and taken a smaller one for a seat. He had before him a stone jug filled with Rhenish wine and two small green wine-glasses. He was alone and only drank out of one glass.

"Will the young gentleman sit down?" he asked in a weak, sibilant voice, beginning at once to cough. "I see the young gentleman is alone, and so am I."

Sten looked interrogatively at the empty glass, but the coughing man answered his question by bringing an unoccupied barrel which he offered him to sit on.

"I have a terrible cough," said the yellow man, "but don't let that disturb you. The spring-time is always trying for those with weak chests. It is now spring again," he added in the melancholy voice with which one might say "It is now autumn again."

Sten felt obliged to say something. "You should drink sweet wine instead of sour."

"My chest complaint is not of that kind," he answered, and began to cough again by way of demonstrating the fact. "I am a clerk in the cloth factory of the town, and there one gets this kind of cough. The dust of the wool affects the lungs and the workers do not live beyond thirty-six. I am now thirty-five," he added with caustic humour, and emptied his glass.

"Why don't you choose another occupation?" asked Sten in a friendly and child-like way.

"Choose? One doesn't choose, young sir. Society in the city is a building in which each man is a stone fitted into its place; if he moves, he disturbs the whole edifice. But society has committed an oversight by not forbidding men in my position to marry. For if the fathers cannot marry till they are thirty and die at thirty-six, the children must go under." He pointed to the ground and continued: "You see, it is a human instinct to climb up; by 'up' one means freedom from work. That is what we climb and struggle for. There are two methods of getting up—an honourable and a dishonourable. The latter is the easier but may end with a crash. I have always been honest."

The drummer standing on the great barrel beat a roll-call on his drum, which signified that someone was about to make a speech.

A heavily built man now mounted a decorated cask. He wore a tunic edged with fur, with a red cloth lining and a round fur cap—a garb which was more adapted for outward appearance than for warmth. It was the mayor.

"Now the King's health will be proposed," explained the factory clerk. "This is the third time that he proposes it, and three times already he has cursed the King and drunk to the health of the Archbishop and the Danish King. A true citizen, you see, drinks to whichever power is in the ascendant, for that power always protects trade, and a city consists of tradesmen; the others do not count."

Sten caught isolated words of the mayor's speech while the clerk continued to whisper in his ear:

"A middleman sits in a comfortable room. He has a letter written to the seller and asks the price. Then he has a letter written to the buyer and asks what he will give. And so the bargain is concluded through him. If the buyer and seller could meet and do their business directly, no middlemen would be necessary, but that they cannot, for then there would be no so-called privileges. And privileges are bestowed by the ruling power."

Outbursts of applause interrupted both the speech of the mayor and the whisperings of the clerk. When the speech was ended all raised their glasses and cried "Long live the King!"—all except the clerk, who stood up and flung his glass against the barrel on which the speaker stood.

An outcry, like a sudden outbreak of fire, rose from the whole company, and in a few seconds the rebellious clerk was carried backwards by strong arms towards the restaurant stairs. There Sten saw him disappear, coughing violently the while. The shrill sound of his cough pierced through the uproar and the roll of the drums which had struck up.

The mayor again desired permission to speak, this time through the city trumpeter, and announced that on this joyous occasion of the King's return, the town and the council would give wine freely. A barrel of wine was rolled along, and placed on a seat amid universal approval.

But now there came a new diversion. From one of the many side-rooms which were generally hired for marriages and other private festivities, came a marriage procession with violin-players and torch-bearers at its head, intending to pass through the great hall and accompany the newly wedded pair home. But that was not possible. The excitement was too great to allow such an opportunity to pass unchallenged.

"Dance the bride's crown off!" was the cry, and the next moment all the young men had formed a circle round the bride, separating her from the bridegroom. The bride was a blooming girl of twenty and the bridegroom was a withered-looking man of thirty with the same sickly pallor as the factory clerk, whom he otherwise somewhat resembled.

Sten's curiosity was directed towards the deserted bridegroom, and he did not understand why he felt a certain sympathy with him, though it was his happiest day. Meanwhile the bride had been blindfolded. Sten was drawn into the ring of dancers, which at one moment circled with dizzying rapidity and at another stood still. The bride stretched out her arms and caught Sten round the neck; he fell on one knee, blushing, kissed her hand, and entered the ring with a garland on his head to dance with the bride, who seemed flattered by such unusual attention. Then he stepped up to the bridegroom, paid him some compliments about his bride, and asked permission to drink to his prosperity. Although it was annoying to the latter to be stopped in this way, he could not refuse, and briefly informed Sten that he also was a clerk in the cloth factory. Sten could not resist giving a start of sympathetic surprise, but had no time to observe the bridegroom more closely, for the latter was now drawn into the ring and had to dance with the bride. Sten underwent a strange sensation and thought of the death-dance depicted on the walls of the chapel of his father's castle. "Poor bridegroom!" he thought, "and poor girl!"

But the joy this evening was quite beyond all bounds, and now tables and seats were cleared away, for the bride's-maids were about to dance the torch-dance, which had been specially called for and which was customary at weddings. The girls received the torches from the bride's escort and invited their cavaliers to dance by handing the torches to them.

Sten had drawn back in order to rest after his exertions, and stood with his back against the cold wall regarding the bridegroom in a melancholy way, as the latter with wine-flushed cheeks fluttered uneasily about the bride, who was surrounded by a number of young men. He felt himself again so lonely among the excited crowd; the various impressions he had undergone during the last twenty-four hours rose up like shadows, and his tired senses began to give way. He closed his eyes and it became dark; the ground seemed to sink under his feet, and he felt a singing in his ears as though he were drowning. He made a supreme effort to hold himself up, and opened his eyes, but saw at first only a dark moving mass in front of him; gradually this was reduced to order and a point of light was kindled against the dark background. It broadened, came nearer, assumed a shape, and then, as when a curtain is quickly drawn back from a picture, a radiant woman's form appeared before him. She was pure light; her eyes were like the Virgin Mary's, her hair resembled silver or gold—it was difficult to say which, her small face was warm and white like newly washed wool. In one hand she held a torch, which she reached to Sten, who took it mechanically, while at the same time he took her free hand which she extended to him. It was all like a vision. As he looked at her small while hand, which lay so confidingly in his, the latter seemed to him, in comparison, like that of the giantess in the bathroom.

Sten had to open the dance. Room was made for them, and he and his partner began to thread the swaying crowd. At one moment they parted from one another, then they met again; one instant he put his arm round her and pressed her to his heart, then another cavalier came and took her from him; but whatever happened, they always met again, and he lighted her way with his uplifted torch. Every time they met again he wished to say something complimentary, but he was dumb and could not utter a word when he looked into her eyes. He was lost in wonder at the whiteness of her hand and the smallness of her foot; the latter peeped forth from under her looped-up dress, and with the well-arched instep was so clearly visible throughout the thin silk shoe that her toes might have been counted. A princess accustomed to walk on roses might have envied the middle-class maiden her foot.

When the dance ceased and Sten had laid down his torch, his partner hesitated for a moment, as though she wished to say something or to ask

Sten to speak. Sten, however, felt as though his tongue were paralysed; but quick as lightning and without considering what he was doing, he embraced her neck and kissed her on both cheeks as one kisses a sister.

There at once arose an uproar among the wedding-guests, and Sten found himself surrounded by threatening hands and angry looks. But the other guests thought the pair so handsome, and Sten looked so innocent as he stood there blushing at his boldness, that they intervened and made peace. The others insisted on a punishment. Then an elderly man, a town-councillor of a cheerful disposition, stepped forward and declared that the offender should be punished on the spot, but that, because of the freedom allowed on this particular day, the law was willing to wink at his offence. On the other hand the insulted maiden, the daughter of a respectable clerk in the public weighing-house, should, if, he added jestingly, she had really been so much insulted, herself adjudicate in the matter. His proposal was accepted with unanimous applause; but Sten felt discomposed to see his princess metamorphosed into a clerk's daughter.

The young girl was embarrassed to the verge of tears, and could not utter a word. At last one of her young friends pressed forward and whispered something in her ear. This advice, whispered at the moment of need, seemed to revive the spirits of the despairing umpire, and with almost inaudible voice she pronounced her verdict "The young gentleman must sing!"

"A song! A song!" shouted the emotional throng, and Sten was condemned to do so. He was lifted by strong arms on to the table and was handed a tortoise-shell lute, which one of the Italian painters, who at that time resided in the city, had brought with him. No one inquired whether the victim could sing, for all assumed that a young man of good family could do so.

Sten first played a prelude on the strings while he recovered himself from his embarrassment and the crowd at his feet heaved like a troubled sea. What should he sing? The smells of beer, wine and fir twigs, mingled with fumes from the oil-lamps and wax-lights, filled the air and made him half unconscious. Before his eyes loomed a chaos of red faces, lamps, casks, instruments and flowers. His fingers wandered over the chords but his ear could not find the tune he wanted. There was silence at last, but the many-headed beast which was now looking up to him so expectantly might, the next moment stir, lose patience, and tear him in pieces. Then he saw the blue eyes and white cheeks which still bore the red marks of his kisses; the strings of the lute sounded, and he felt chorda in his breast which responded. After striking some loud notes, he began, in a weak voice which grew stronger as he went on, a song in the style of the old Minnesingers, and when he had concluded it he was fully acquitted by the audience. Then the good-natured councillor stepped up to him, thanked him, put his arm round his neck, and walked with him into one of the side-rooms. Here he placed him on a seat, and standing before him with folded arms, he assumed a judicial tone and said: "That was the song, young gentleman; now let us have the words! You have some trouble on your mind, you are not on the right road, and you steal into the town without a pass—you see, we watch our people and they are not too many to be counted."

Sten was beside himself with alarm, but the councillor quieted him, asked him to relate his story, and promised to be his friend. When Sten perceived that the facts must come out in any case, he chose the present favourable opportunity to narrate them privately to a friendly person, knowing that perhaps to-morrow, when the effects of wine had ceased to work, his friendliness might have evaporated. Accordingly he frankly told the councillor everything.

When he had ended, the latter said, "Well, you are looking for an occupation which is suited to your strength and capacity. You can write, and, as it happens, the city just needs a clerk, for a place will be vacant this evening."

"In the cloth factory?" asked Sten, with a gloomy foreboding that the answer would be in the affirmative.

"Yes."

"The unfortunate man has then been dismissed for his imprudence?"

"Naturally! The city is the key of the kingdom; those who guard the key-cupboard must not be surrounded by traitors."

"I cannot accept the post," declared Sten, remembering the kindness which the unfortunate man had shown him. "'One man dead gives another man bread!'"

"You are ashamed of walking over corpses? But what is our pilgrimage here but a fight for life or death, or a lyke-wake where one sits and waits till the body is carried out. How did I become a councillor? By waiting for the deaths of six others. How shall I become mayor? By waiting for the present mayor's death. And that may be a long time," he added with a sigh. "As regards the dismissed man, I am very sorry for him, but am glad at the same time that you will be saved from going under."

"But he has wife and children."

"Very sad for them! But when a man has renounced his place, as he has done, it is vacant; if you refuse to take it, you will be doing neither him nor yourself a service. Between ourselves, we all thought somewhat as he did, but, look you! one must not say so. I am an old man, sir, and have seen life. It is a perverse and mad business, and Satan himself cannot help one. At present your velvet jacket is white, but to-morrow it will be dirty; the day after, it will be torn, and then, do you know what you are? No longer a young gentleman, but an adventurer and a tramp. Hear my advice, young man. Get bread for your mouth so long as your velvet jacket lasts, and hold your tongue. Sleep over the matter and come on Monday morning to the town hall. I wish you good night and common sense."

Sten rose and returned to the great hall. But it seemed to him empty and desolate now that the bridal procession had vanished. Tired and exhausted by the various emotions he had undergone during the evening and the past twenty-four hours, he resolved to go home.

When he came to the inn and entered his room, he took off his velvet jacket and inspected it. Stained with wine, dirty with the dust of the high road, browned with sweat under the arm-pits, it looked wretched enough. He lay down and went to sleep wondering where the weighing-house might be; he dreamt of death-dances and factory clerks, fought with corpses, and awoke. Then he went to sleep again thinking of the weighing-house and of a tender farewell to the velvet jacket, with a firm resolve to earn bread, first for one month, and then for two.

The beautiful month of May did not keep its promises; snow fell while the apple trees were in blossom, and the sun did not appear for fourteen days. For fourteen dreadful days had Sten, the last scion of the family of Ulffot at Wäringe, Hofsta and Löfsala, stood at his post in the draughty, unwarmed factory by the harbour. From morning till late in the evening he had stood there, with a pen in his half-frozen fingers, registering the names of the kinds of cloth which had been brought by the incoming vessels. He did not really understand why they should be registered any more than if they had been so many stones of the street, flakes of snow, or drops of water; but he obeyed the old councillor's advice, and held his tongue whenever he felt tempted to ask.

The room where he worked was continually being entered by porters and merchants who left snow and dirt on the floor, and let the cold air blow in freely. One bale of cloth after another was thrown upon an enormous table and filled the air with a choking dust. He had not yet begun to cough, but he felt that he breathed with more difficulty; and to add to his troubles, the intense cold had burnt holes in his white hands and made them quite red.

One day he went to a barber's and looked at himself in a mirror. He thought it was another person he was looking at when he saw a lean yellow face full of spots and fringed with an untidy beard. His feet had become so swollen that he could not wear his ordinary boots, but had to use Lapland shoes. He had changed his white jacket for a brown frock-coat and his cap for a slouched hat. His scanty pay obliged him to take his meals in third-rate restaurants where he only got salted food, and the unaccustomed diet had brought on an attack of scurvy. When he once ventured to complain to one of his senior fellow-workers, the latter took him to task and said there were many who worked more than Sten and got no food at all; he himself had had no fresh food since Christmas. This man was the bridegroom whom Sten had met in the restaurant of the town hall; he was envious of Sten because the latter, while still so young, had obtained a post for which he had been waiting for ten years.

"Many get everything given them in this life, and yet are not satisfied," he often remarked when consoling Sten. The latter envied hint because of his comparatively good health, his uninjured hands and feet, and the indifference with which he took things. He on his part declared that Sten suffered because he had been spoilt and had not learned to work, and from this opinion he would not budge.

Sten felt that his bodily health was giving way under the struggle; his friend said that it was a fall in an honourable battle of which no knight need be ashamed. Sten thought that his soul was being injured by the murderous work of perpetually writing figures; however, his friend asserted it was not the fault of the work but because he had been badly educated.

Badly educated! He who had had two nurses and a governess, he who had had tutors in Greek and Latin, could play the lute, and make fine verses! That he would not acknowledge. But he knew that he was unhappy. He also knew now where the weighing-house was. But what was the use of that? He had seen the young girl at a Mass in the city church, but she had been shocked at his appearance; and his friend in the cloth factory told him that she thought Sten looked degenerated. His friend also told him that her father had some money, gave his daughter an education, and hoped to get her well married, so that it was not worth while for Sten to wear out his boots by going there, he added.

One day Sten, weary of copying figures, felt he had had enough of the dark room. Better, he thought, any physical exertion than this eternal writing in which there was no progress and no end. He resigned his post. It was in the middle of a hot summer. He wandered up and down the streets without object and without hope. Lost in thoughts, he contemplated the houses and their signboards as though he expected to find there the answer to the riddle of his life. His gaze was arrested by a large horseshoe which hung on a pole; memories of a nag and a highway began to stir in his brain. Then he heard the blows of a hammer in the courtyard. He entered in and saw a giant who was forging horseshoes. The work proceeded slowly and the giant panted and sweated at each blow.

It brightened Sten up to see the sparks dancing round the anvil, and the forge also diffused a cheerful glow. But the smith did not seem in a cheerful mood, for he broke off his work, sat down on a log of wood, and watched with gloomy looks the iron growing cold. Then as though stung by an evil conscience he went into the smithy and came out again with a piece of red-hot iron, but seemed to be still more depressed, for he laid the iron on the anvil, and then sat down and watched it as though he expected it to turn into horseshoes. Presently he turned round, and Sten, seeing his face, recognised Claus. He went up to him and greeted him as an old acquaintance. Claus at first regarded him with astonishment, and after he had been obliged to recognise him, maintained an air of severe coldness. Suddenly his face brightened, as though a thought had struck him.

"Listen!" he said. "Are you free at present?"

Sten replied that he certainly was.

"By Saint Anschar, you shall become a smith! Now I see that you were really born to be one. Strange what mistakes one may make sometimes! You have developed a pair of fists since we last met, and one soon learns how to grasp a hammer!"

"It is certainly too hard for me, since I did not begin it when I was young," objected Sten.

"Hard? What the dickens! It is not harder than anything else—I mean for one who has the capacity. Listen! We will be good friends and have a fine time. The master sits the whole day in the beer-shop, and only you and I will be here."

Sten thought the proposal as good as any he was likely to meet with, and believed he would find a support in Claus. Accordingly he consented.

"Then we will go at once to the master of the guild of smiths at the journeymen's inn," said Claus.

Sten reminded him that he had said he occupied this office of master, but Claus replied he had given it up owing to having too much to do. They went therefore to the master, whose reception of Claus was so obviously disdainful that Sten on the spot lost a considerable amount of the respect he had felt for him. Meanwhile he was enrolled as an apprentice of the guild, and this new dignity of his was sealed by their drinking a number of mugs of beer in a public-house, and in the evening was ratified by Claus's master, who was the worse for drink. Sten slept that night at the smithy.

The next morning, while the matin-bell was ringing in the Ave Maria Convent, Sten was aroused by being violently shaken by Claus, who said: "Light the fire in the forge and tell me when it burns. I am going to doze a little longer."

Sten blew the fire and worked the bellows for half an hour. When at last it burnt up brightly, he woke Claus.

"Now put the iron in, and tell me when it gets red, I want still to have a wink or two," said Claus, turning to the wall.

When the iron was glowing as red as blood, Sten woke him again.

"Now hammer out the iron till it is as slender as a finger, while I shake off my sleepiness," said Claus, yawning.

Sten went back to the smithy, but now the iron had become black. He worked the bellows and made it red again. Then he took it up with the tongs and carried it out to the anvil, but before he had seized the sledge-hammer, it was once more black. This process was repeated till Sten became tired. Then he returned to Claus, who was snoring loud, and had drawn his leather apron over his head in order not to be disturbed by the daylight.

Claus became impatient. "Well, you stupid, can't you take the hammer in one hand and the tongs in the other?"

Sten replied he could not.

"Then you can go for a jug of beer."

Sten felt ashamed of going into the street with a tin can, but as Claus began to search in a tool-chest for a hammer, he hurried out.

The morning was fine; the sun shone on the gable-roofs of the houses, and women and girls were proceeding to market. When Sten came out of the public-house with the beer, and was about to cross the street, he suddenly stopped, as though riveted, before someone who gazed at him in astonishment and sorrow. He wished to turn round, but the crowd prevented him; he wanted to raise his cap, but the beer-jug required both his black hands to hold it.

The girl went on her way, and Sten hastened, weeping, back to the smithy.

"What are you whimpering for?" said Claus, who had shaken off his sleep and come out into the sunshine, where he drank his morning draught.

Sten did not answer. Claus took out a plank which he laid on the wooden log against the wall of the house so that he had a support for his back.

"Now we will work," he said, crossing his arms and making himself as comfortable as possible. "You will begin with the cold iron first, so that you learn how to handle the hammer."

Sten lifted the hammer, which was very heavy for him. He struck on the anvil while Claus counted "One and two! and one and two! and one and two!"

"Yes, yes; now you see what a workman has to do. One and two! and one and two! and—— That is something different from lying on eider-down and eating roast-veal! And two and—— You think one gets accustomed to have the sun on one's neck, the forge in one's face, and the smoke in one's nose? No, look you, one never does. And what do you think a pretty girl says when a smith comes with his black hands and wants to put his arm round her waist? 'Let me alone, lout!' she says. A smith can certainly marry when he has saved some money, but he must take an ugly girl whom no one else will have. And two! and one!—— Are you listening? Do you remember when you sat in the inn and ate fowl with sage stuffing, and, I had a salted herring in my bag? And he had a horse, the young devil, and a velvet jacket. Where is the horse now? Perhaps he is standing in the stable in the Knacker's House, or whatever your father's castle was called. Do you remember that I made you believe that Sir Vulcan was councillor to the Emperor of Rome. Ha! ha! No, a smith is a smith, that is all."

Sten was growing tired.

"Are you lazy, you devil?" said Claus.

"Stop calling me devil," said Sten, "I am not accustomed to it."

"Perhaps his Grace is used to being called 'angel'?" said Claus scornfully.

Sten *had* been once used to it, but he refrained from saying so. He went on with his hammer strokes.

"One and two! and one and two! and one—— No," said Claus, "you can do that now. Beat out the iron rod now; it is harder to do when it is cold, but still it can be done. I must go now to some business in the town, and when the old man comes, tell him that I met my brother-in-law from the country. But if you have not beaten out the iron rod by the time I come back, I will weld your hind legs together, so that you will be like a herring."

Sten felt quite exhausted and declared that he could not finish the work alone. He also said openly that he had not come here to do Claus's work while the latter sat in the ale-house.

Claus became furious. "Yes, you have, my young man," he shouted. "That is just what you have come for. Look you! I have worked for thirty-five years, and you have done nothing; now I am the nobleman and let you work for me! Is it not so with the aristocracy?" Claus leant himself against the plank with his arms folded and continued: "Yes, I am a devilish fine nobleman, you can believe me! And you will see how I shall flourish. I shall not be rich, but I shall be fat. You look disapproving. You don't agree with my plan, nor understand it. The upper class have invented it themselves, and a very excellent one it is."

Sten replied that in his opinion Claus was a bumpkin.

"Go and fetch the big hammer. You will do some extra work by way of punishment," Claus replied haughtily.

Sten's blood boiled over and he raised the iron rod against Claus. At the same moment he felt something give way in his body, and fell senseless to the ground.

When Sten awoke to consciousness he was lying in a bed at the hospital, and was condemned to inaction for several months, for he had broken a blood-vessel, and his recovery was doubtful. In the large ward one bed stood close to another, and as soon as it was empty there was always someone waiting to occupy it. Here he saw every day instances how those who did physical labour were exposed to accidents which other classes escaped. At one time it was a carpenter who had cut his foot; at another a mason who had fallen from a scaffolding. One day came a breweress who had scalded herself when boiling wort; on another a pewterer who had burnt his knee at the smelting oven.

Hitherto he had had no idea how widely spread human sufferings were, and when he contrasted his past with his present, he began to guess how the legend of the rich man, who could not enter heaven, had arisen. Thus he lay the whole summer, without fresh air or seeing anything green. He felt bitterly how the best time of the year was passing, and imagined how it looked in the country, and what people were doing every day. Numbers of monks came to the ward, and almost every day the crucifix was lifted by some bed-side to comfort a sufferer.

Sten often talked with the monks and he could not help sharing their view that the earth was a vale of tears. When his pains became severe he felt relief in contemplating the Crucified Who writhed on the cross, and he understood now why the Christian creed had been able to gain so many disciples. One day, when he was especially suffering, he had a visit from Claus, who had heard a report that Sten was dying. He felt now compelled to see and speak with the sick man, and, if possible, to comfort him; but in order to strengthen himself he went first into an ale-shop, with the result that he reached the hospital in a somewhat hilarious condition.

When he again met Sten, whose face had recovered its fair complexion and his hands their delicacy, his former respect for him awoke, and he confessed to himself that there were a finer and a coarser kind of men. He called Sten "sir," and advised him to think about his soul and to repent of his sins; he should not, he said, be sorry that he had to die, for the smiths' company would carry him to the grave, and afterwards hold such a funeral feast as had never been seen in the city. Then he threw out some delicate hints that it was a pity for the hospital to get Sten's clothes when he was dead, and at the same time expressed his admiration of the excellent wool of which Sten's coat was made; for the rest, he believed that old trousers could be altered, and told Sten above all things to take care that nothing was left in the pockets. Life, he said, was very troublesome, and parents who did not teach their children to work with their hands were worse than murderers, and to give children an education was to spoil them. Sten would have made a good smith, if he had learnt to wield the hammer from his childhood, and he might by this time have married the maiden from the weighing-house. As it was, she had engaged herself to one of the yeomen of the guard. Sten, however, should not be sad about that, for he had not much longer to live, but Claus would carry the flag at his funeral procession as a token that he had forgiven the young gentleman all the wrong he had done him. As he uttered these last words, Claus was so overcome by his noble sentiments that he wept as only a drunken man can.

But Claus never carried the flag, because he was not the guild's flag-bearer, and because Sten recovered. One fine autumn day he was dismissed from the hospital and told that he was no longer ill, but that he would never be strong enough to work. Now he realised the whole terrible truth of what Claus had said: his education had robbed him of the means of earning a livelihood. It was in vain that he went about and sought a place in an already organised society; there was no place for drones in this hive. The only thing remaining was to flee from this hive and seek another where the working-bees supported the drones. He thought of the convents where men did not work but lived very comfortably and could devote their leisure to such refined enjoyments as arts and sciences, and he wondered that he had not before this enlisted in the armies of the Church.

With a light step he walked down to the convent of the Dominican monks in the Osterlang-gata, and rang the bell. The little window in the gate was opened and a monk asked Sten his name and address. He gave his name and asked to speak to the prior with a view to entering the convent. The gate was opened and Sten was admitted into the garden, where he was told to wait.

Meanwhile the prior sat in the hall of the chapter going through the estate and rent books with the steward. Various deficits in these showed a serious diminution in the income of the convent. They were just consulting how this might be increased to its highest possible point again, as the General Chapter of the Dominican Order was constantly demanding support for the war against the heretics, when the gate-keeper's assistant announced Sten Ulffot's arrival, name, and business.

"Ulffot of Wäringe, Hofsta and Löfsala," the prior said to himself, and made the sign of the cross. "He comes as opportunely as though he were sent by St Dominic himself. I know Löfsala thoroughly; it is a splendid estate—twelve hundred acres of open ground, besides saleable meadows and woods, water-mills, saw-mills and a splendid eel-fishery. Let him in! Let him in by all means! Bid the gentleman welcome in the name of the Lord."

"Your Reverence," interposed the steward, "wait a minute. Löfsala is a fine estate certainly, but sad to say the present owner has no taste for the spiritual life."

"The present owner?"

"Yes, the Ulffot family," continued the steward, "has been obliged to give up everything, and the last member of it is said to be an adventurer who has tried a little of everything but carried nothing out, and is quite come down in the world."

"What do you say? What do you say? H'm! Well, what shall we do with him?"

"From him we shall get neither profit nor honour," said the steward. "We have monks enough who eat our provisions, and this is not a poorhouse."

"Quite right!" said the prior. "Quite right! But who is to tell him that? One of St Dominic's wisest and best rules is, never to send anyone unsatisfied away. Will Brother Francis go into the garden and speak a little with the young man? Speak a little with him, explain it to him, you understand! Let us go on with our work, steward."

Brother Francis was a tall man, of alarming appearance, with a bearish temper, who was employed to scare away such applicants as were not "edible," in the phraseology of the industrious brotherhood; for the Dominican Order was a powerful political corporation, which lived in perpetual strife with princes, for power and property, and was by no means an institution for exercising benevolence.

When Brother Francis saw Sten's insignificant appearance he thought he could make short work with him. "What do you want in the convent?" he asked without any preliminary remarks.

"I seek for the peace which the world cannot give," answered Sten.

"Then you have come to the wrong place," said Francis. "This is the armoury of the Church Militant, and there is never peace here."

"Peace follows fighting," Sten ventured to object; but this irritated the monk, who wished to get done with a thankless task.

"Say what you want and speak the truth—something like this: 'I cannot dig and to beg I am ashamed; therefore I will come here and eat.' If you say that, you will not be lying."

Sten felt that the monk had to a certain extent hit the mark, and answered simply, "Alas, you are right!"

Surprised at this unexpected admission, and touched by Sten's childlikeness, the monk took him farther into the garden and continued his talk. "I know your history and understand the riddle of your life. When Nature is left to herself, she produces masterpieces; but when man interferes with her work, he makes a bungle of it. Look at this pear tree; it is a descendant from a pear tree at Santa Lucia in Spain, where it was cultivated for five hundred years. You think it is an excellent thing that it can bring forth fine fruits to please our palates? Nature does not think so, for she has produced the fruit for the sake of the pipe which continue the species. Look at this pear when I cat it in two! Do you see any pips? No! Over-cultivation has done away with them. Look at this apple which glows so magnificently with red and gold! It is an English pearmain. It has pips, but if I sow them they produce crab-apples. When, however, a severe winter comes, the pearmain trees are killed by frost, but the crab-apple trees are not. Therefore one ought to give up over-cultivating people, especially when it is done at the expense of others. Such cultivation is unsuited to our country and our severe climate. Have I expressed myself clearly? I am sorry for you, young man, but I cannot help you. *Beati possidentes*—blessed are those who have succeeded. Your ancestors won success, but they had not the skill to maintain it!"

He went on to talk of indifferent matters while he conducted Sten to the gate. "There will be an early winter this year, if we may judge by the ash-berries." Then he opened the gate, bowed politely and said "Good-bye, sir."

When the gate closed, Sten felt that he was shut out from society once for all, and he rallied the small remainder of bodily and mental strength which he possessed, to form a resolution. But his will and thinking power bed collapsed. The twilight had fallen. He followed the descent of the steep street which led to the sea, as though he were obeying the law of gravitation. His feet led him into a narrow alley which was quite dark and filled with an overpowering stench from the offal which had been thrown away there; but he went on and on, guided by a faint light which appeared at the bottom of the alley. Presently he stood before a water-gate which had been left ajar and through which a moonbeam pierced the darkness. He opened the gate and before him lay the surface of the water lit by the moon which was rising over the island of Sikla. The little waves danced and played in the path of the moonlight and the sea breeze blew freshly shore-wards.

Sten stepped over the narrow threshold and let the gate close behind him, without exactly thinking what he was doing. At the same moment all the bells in the city began to ring for vespers, and the drummers on the city walls beat the tattoo as a signal for the citizens to go to bed. Sten took off his cap, fell on his knees, and said a prayer. Then he stood up, turned his back towards the sea, folded his arms over his breast, looked up at the stars and let himself fall backwards, as though he were going to rest. The silvery water mirror opened like a dark grave, which closed again at once, and a great ring, like a halo, appeared on the surface; it widened into many more circles, which dispersed and died away. Soon the little waves reappeared and danced and played in the moonlight as though they had never been frightened.

"UNWELCOME"

The baptism service was over, and the family party had got into the boats and hoisted sail. The little fleet now glided out of the green bay below the island chapel. In the first boat sat the god-parents with the newly baptised infant.

"It was a strange idea to call the boy 'Christian,'" said the mother's sister to the father's sister, as she put the child's feeding-bottle to its mouth.

"Oh, it doesn't matter what one is called, and if he has the same name as the Danish King it is good enough," said the other.

"Yes, but the poor boy will have no name-day if he has no patron saint."

"That is all right, for then no one will have the trouble of celebrating it. He was not wished for and he was hardly welcome," said the father's sister.

In the second boat sat the father and mother and the two elder children, a boy and a girl aged seven and eight respectively.

"We could have done very well without another one," said the father as he ported the helm.

"It is all very well talking now," said his wife as she counter-braced the sail.

"Yes, I know," he replied.

"But you will be kind to him?" she said.

"I must be, I suppose," was his answer. He pushed his boy down from the boat-side on which he had clambered, saying, "Keep still in the boat, children, or the devil will have you."

In the third boat sat the pastor and the grand-parents.

"How is the fishing?" asked the former.

"So-so," answered the grandfather. "The Lord knows where the fish go now. When I was young, one caught enough herrings in two nights to last the winter, and now it is doubtful whether one catches any at all."

"Yes, it is strange; I had three standing nets out there on Wednesday night and did not catch a fin," said the pastor. "Winter will bring hard times, and one ought to look forward before producing more mouths than one can fill."

"I told him so," said the grandfather assentingly. "The house is big enough for one brood, not for two. Better one farmer than two cottagers. I don't think, however, he will divide the farm, but this last child must go out into service like others."

"That is certainly as good as starving at home," said the pastor.

The July sun blazed hotly upon the fjord, the sky was perfectly blue, and the newly baptised child screamed, whether from joy or grief it was difficult to say. Soon the thatched roofs of the farm were visible among the alders, and the boats halted at the bridge. The occupants disembarked and were regaled with a good meal spread under the oak trees. Afterwards the pastor thanked God for the happiness with which he had blessed the house, and bade the guests raise their glasses to welcome the new citizen of the world into the congregation.

Christian grew up among the calves and pigs, for his brother and sister were too old to play with him. He seemed born with two characteristics which never left him: one was to be always in the way, the other was to be never welcome. Wherever he appeared, behind a bush, on a haystack, under a boat, in a loft, or in the cottage, the cry always was, "Is it you, young scoundrel?" Wherever he happened to be, and anyone approached, they said, "You always have to be in the way."

His parents, who for eight years had been unaccustomed to the crying of a baby, and were now a good deal older so that they enjoyed a good sleep, found it somewhat difficult to reconcile themselves to his crying at night, and they soon came to regard it as a failing which was peculiar to their youngest born. It was in vain that the grandmother asserted that all children cried, and that Hans the eldest had really cried much more when he was little. His father said he could not remember that at all; all he remembered was that Hans had been an uncommonly good child, who had always been a source of joy to his parents. There was such a great difference, he added, between children.

Meanwhile Christian, who was intelligent enough to see that he was in the way, acquired the habit of keeping out of the way; when he saw anyone he hid himself, ran out to the woods and fields, and was up to all kinds of mischief.

As he became older and was strong enough to do some useful work, attempts were made to tame him, but in vain. When put in charge of cattle, he ran away from them and let them go into the fields; he laid the fishing-nets so deep that they could not be got up again, and when sought for, he was not to be found. In short he seemed half a savage. Once, at his elder brother's suggestion, he was beaten, but then he remained away eight whole days, and when he reappeared he was as stout and strong as before; no one knew what he had eaten or where he had slept.

But Christian himself knew well enough. The scanty diet of his home consisted chiefly of salt fish, turnips and bread. Christian, who often had to satisfy himself with what fell from the table, or was left over, often felt a longing for more nourishing food, especially as he grew older and approached manhood. He was hungry the whole day, and went to the wood and the seashore to get food. Fish did not attract him, for he had chewed them till he was tired and they gave him no strength; he looked for warm-blooded creatures, and when he caught some young birds he ate them raw. Then he felt stronger as the blood diffused an intoxicating warmth throughout his body. Eggs had the same effect; these he took ruthlessly from the nests of the sea-birds on the shore. In this way he procured for himself a diet which was much more nourishing than his parents and brother and sister could contrive to obtain.

So he grew, and became strong, but could not make up his mind to work. In a rude boat which he had managed to construct himself, he cruised about the islands and hunted for eggs. His parents, who did not exactly miss his presence, soon began to regard him as having flown from the nest.

One fine spring day, when the eider-geese were flying over the outermost islands, Christian sailed out with his bow and his nooses, more for the sake of amusement and passing the time than for practical purposes, for he never killed anything except for immediate consumption. He landed with his boat on one of those skerries which form the last breakwater against the open sea, and which only sea-birds and fishermen frequent during the summer. The skerry was uninhabited, but a rude shed had been built on it to serve as a sleeping-place for fishermen in the fishing season, and as a shelter for travellers and those who might be driven ashore. It consisted of a single room with the bare earth for its floor; along the wall were arranged berths like shelves furnished with sheep-skins for sleeping under. Two stones on the ground marked where a fire might be lit, and flint and steel were kept in a place well known to all between the beams above the door. The door was always closed but could be opened with a bent wooden peg. Everyone had a right to enter if they only closed the door after them and put back the flint and steel in its place. If any-body wished to show benevolence or gratitude, they placed an armful of grass or juniper twigs near the fire-place, for there was not a tree on the skerry. It was in these shelters that Christian generally slept, and there he took his simple meals; he knew each one of them for miles around, and where the best sheep-skins were to be found. The fleas which infested them generally left him alone.

Meanwhile the spring evening was beautiful, and the sea lay there serene in blue tranquillity. Christian, who had learnt not to trust it, drew his boat up and hid it behind some great stones. He had rowed far and clambered about on the rocks, so that he went into the rest-house and got into the topmost berth to sleep. He lay there for a time and thought about various things—about the day which had just passed, about his life and its purposes, and the life which should follow this. He had opened the sky-light and saw the steel-grey heaven above him, and a star or two which palely glimmered in the lingering sunlight. Has religious instincts had not been educated either by parents, pastors or teachers, nor had he been confirmed, but he knew that behind nature and the events of life were guiding powers of which one had no nearer knowledge. He had arrived at no certainty regarding the object of his existence. Together with the gift of life, he had received the instinct to preserve it, and obeyed this instinct. What more was there to do? He ate in order to be able to work, and worked in order to get something to eat. Yes, but in the intervals, he thought, or, rather, he wondered. He wondered whether perhaps these very thoughts of his constituted the higher aim of life of which he dreamt; he remembered that his mother had said that the earth was a vale of tears through which we must wander in order to become better and thereby worthier of the Kingdom of Heaven. He found, on closer reflection, that he neither grew better nor worse from one day to another, and he did not understand how he was to improve. Perhaps he was an exception? Possibly. All others took the oath of loyalty to the King; all others paid taxes, went to church, paid tithes to the clergy, paid rent, swept the snow away for one another, bought and sold, summoned each other before the law-courts, but could do nothing without asking permission and payment. They asked permission to be able to marry, to be received into the community where they were born, to be buried in the earth; and on each occasion there were fees to pay. They paid the King for ruling them, they paid the judge for judging them, the pastor for saving them, and the executioner for hanging them; they paid in the town for the right to sell their fish, and they paid for the bridges on which the town's existence depended. Christian, who did nothing of all this, was therefore an exception, and the reason he escaped all these payments was, that he possessed nothing. That was the difference between him and them: he possessed nothing. In earlier times he had heard those who had nothing sailed out on the sea and took from those who had. This was now not permitted, and rightly so, for Christian could not think it permissible that anyone should come and take his boat or his axe from him.

While these half-developed thoughts came and went in the half-consciousness of a tired brain, sleep overcame him. After some hours he awoke with a choking feeling in his chest and a terrible smarting in his eyes. He sat up in his berth and saw that a fire had been made on the ground below. By it sat two men—one in the half-barbaric costume of the inhabitants of Dägo, the other in the everyday garb of a Swedish fisherman. They were roasting some herrings before the fire. Christian, who did not feel inclined to move, as he did not know how the strangers might be disposed, protected himself from the smoke as well as he could by creeping as far as possible under the coverlet; he did not blame himself for listening to their conversation, but, as we shall see afterwards, turned it to profit.

"They are a stupid lot, these Swedes!" said the man from Dägo, who believed that his superior bodily strength gave him the right to say what he liked.

"Oh, you mustn't talk ill of the Swedes," said the other, who in such a nocturnal *tête-à-tête* did not venture to use a more impolite form of speech.

"Well, can one imagine less enterprising people than these fishermen? If they knew what the eider-birds' down was worth in Russia, they would be able to make a pile of money."

"Yes, but you see the Swedes think it wrong to deprive the birds of the down which they need for hatching their eggs."

"That is just their stupidity; for if they don't take it, foreigners will, like they take everything else."

"No, it is not stupidity, it is consideration to think of our successors, who also should derive profit from the birds which would disappear, if disturbed."

"That is not true; but if foreigners came, they would take both eggs and down together."

"They can do that if they have no conscience; Swedes would rather be poor than behave so badly."

"That is why I call them stupid. But now, to speak of another matter. Why don't you hunt ermines and squirrels here as they do inland?"

"Because we have enough to do with the fish and prefer the certain to the uncertain."

"That is right; but I should prefer a sure income from skins and down to an insecure one from the sea. If I had nothing else to do, it wouldn't be long before I had enough money to buy a piece of ground to build upon and fish too."

The Swede dropped the subject and shared his food with the stranger, who had anchored before the skerry because the wind had fallen. When it rose again at sunrise they both left the rest-house, little guessing what seeds they had sown in Christian's uncultured brain.

No sooner had the sound of their footsteps died away than he sprang up and went out. The rifling sun illumined the open sea which was ruffled by the morning breeze, and over whose surface sea-birds were circling. To Christian this scene was not new, but to-day the sun seemed to shine more brightly and his horizon was enlarged. His eye, which had often swept the surface of the water without finding an object behind the blue line which bound the horizon, fancied it perceived, hidden by the clouds in the east, a distant land where the deliverer dwelt who would come and make him like other men; he would cease to be in the way; he would be welcome somewhere, would rest upon his own roof, and perhaps possess a small spot on this earth where he hitherto was hunted about like a trespassing dog. Hope awoke in his soul, and when he saw the strange boat hoist sail and enter the golden path traced on the waves by the sun, he fancied himself standing by the helm and steering to the distant land behind the blue horizon with his precious cargo, and now he determined to begin a new life.

Far out in the Fjallang Fjord, almost in the open sea, lies a skerry which is called Trollhattorna or the "Goblin's Cap." It consists of a round crag with four flat sides which have a certain resemblance to the cape which the goblins of fairy-tales are supposed to wear. Between these faces of the crag are deep clefts where guillemots build their nests, and where they are completely protected from rain and wind. After sundry combats with the fearless owners Christian had succeeded in obtaining undisturbed possession of that cleft which faced the land, into which the wind from the sea never blew. Here he had contrived a storehouse for his collected treasures by stretching a rain-proof sealskin, which he occasionally smeared with train-oil, between the walls of the cleft. He spent two years in amassing these treasures, and employed in doing so all his long-trained capacities. He could imitate all creatures' voices; he could whistle like the weasel, make a smacking noise like the squirrel, and grumble like the eider-duck. He knew how to approach one of the latter when sitting on her nest of seaweed on the open beach, and he could look at her so that she quietly let him stroke her back while he plucked the down. He never took more than one of the six eggs, and if the nestlings were already hatched he left them in peace; the ermine he sometimes caught with traps and sometimes shot them with blunted arrows so that the fur should not be injured. Squirrels he watched for from behind an oak, and could entice them to come so near that he could seize them with his hands; in the winter he dragged them by the help of a willow branch from their nests, and obtained their entire store of hazel-nuts besides.

His senses had grown so fine by practice that he could hear a mile off what sort of bird was approaching, and even in the twilight he could distinguish at an incredible distance between a black water-hen and a merganser. Among his worst rivals, the crows, who hunted the eider-ducks in order to devour their eggs, he did great execution. By exposing the bodies of weasels and squirrels which he had skinned, he allured whole swarms of these uninvited plunderers, which he then shot down. Such was his skill and so completely undisturbed was he, that within two years he had accumulated in his grotto a store which seemed to him sufficient to bring him to the foreign land where the sun rose, and where people would know how to appreciate his treasures. Now again the spring was approaching, and the thought how he should construct a vessel sufficiently large and seaworthy began to disquiet him.

He knew that he could get out to the open sea very easily with a large fishing-boat such as was used for catching herrings, and that it was not more than two days' journey to the land on the other side, but he saw small prospect of being able to build such a boat and of procuring the expensive sails. His natural instinct, which revolted against the idea of anyone coming and taking from him what he had earned by his own work, forbade his procuring such a boat in any unlawful way.

The spring came nearer and nearer, and his disquietude increased. One afternoon he was sitting on the highest point of Trollhattorna, looking out over the sea where sails appeared and disappeared. A red-brown eider-duck came swimming with its young ones after it; the sea-gulls flew past his ears screaming, and the mergansers answered them. Christian felt like a mountain king as he sat there above his treasure-chamber, but at the same time he seemed to himself to have been bewitched by the mountain spirits, for he saw no prospect of getting away. Just then he heard the measured stroke of oars behind him, and saw a boat with four men in it being rowed towards the place where he sat. As it came nearer, he recognised his father and brother, but did not know the two others, one of whom shouted to him: "Come down, you pirate!"

Christian remained where he was.

"Obey, when the King's sheriff orders you," said his father.

High up on the skerry stood a pile of stones which the fishermen had set there as a mark. Christian was prepared to defend himself. "I am not a pirate," he said.

"Ah, do you contradict the King's sheriff," said his father. "Beware! and do not make us all miserable."

"I make no one miserable," answered Christian, "but I defend myself when I see that people wish me ill. What do you want from me?"

"You have here a hiding-place for goods which you have stolen from peaceful traders," said the sheriff. "We have seen all."

"I have stolen nothing from anyone," said Christian. "All that is here I have earned by hard work."

"Nonsense! Do you think we shall believe that one can collect so many skins and all this down here in these bare skerries. Come down, for the last time, or we will take you."

They began to climb the cliff, but then Christian began to hurl down blocks of stone, which bounded over the heads of his assailants, knocked splinters out of the rocks, and plumped into the water, without however striking anyone.

"Wretched boy!" cried his father. "You were born for my ruin!"

"Who begot me?" answered Christian, and threw the last stone.

Now the besiegers had a prospect of success, and soon Christian felt his legs caught in a noose; and he was soon wound up like a ball, rolled down the hill, and laid in the bottom of the boat.

"Do not hurt him unnecessarily," said his father. "I will be security for him."

Then he began in a comparatively friendly tone to tell Christian how badly he had treated his parents, who had produced him, clothed him, and been kind to him; with what sorrow and shame he had requited them since their name would now become notorious and dishonoured in the neighbourhood. He adjured him by the Cross of Christ and all the saints that he should confess his sin, since by his doing so the offence would be half pardoned and might be atoned for by a fine. He pointed to his grey hairs and begged Christian not to bring dishonour on them; he bade him to think of his brother who would soon take his father's place and uphold the good name and prosperity of the family; he concluded by declaring that one must not live for oneself but for others also, because society was built up of families, and if families did not hold together, society would fall. Christian should therefore acknowledge his crime.

But Christian had committed no crime, and therefore could not save society. His father's unwonted mildness moved him and he wished for a moment that he had done what he was accused of.

Their talk continued till they reached home. Christian was taken to the barn and locked up there. The others went to the cottage, where they ate their supper and talked over the matter. Presently, as Christian lay reflecting on the floor of the barn, the door opened, and his mother stepped in.

"Son," she said, "think of your old mother, and tell the truth."

"Then mother would rather have a thief for her son than an honourable boy?"

"I want you to confess; then your father will pay a fine for your offence, and our good name will be saved."

"That is strange," said Christian, whose brain could not follow this line of thought. "If I make myself a criminal, then the crime can be pardoned, but if I continue to be honourable, it cannot. What crime? One which has never been committed? For I have not stolen; I have only gone where anyone can go, and for a long time have collected skins and eggs as I have leave to do."

But his mother replied that that had nothing to do with it; the one thing necessary was that he should confess, since; the King's sheriff desired it.

His mother departed sadly. Then came his sister, and said that Christian should not plunge her too into misery; for if the family were disgraced, her fiancé, Peter, could not marry her. Christian had only to confess, then he would be free and his father would pay the fine.

Christian replied that he could not say "yes" when he ought to say "no."

But why, she rejoined, could he not when he would make so many people happy?

Oh, did his sister then wish him to lie?

Why should he not under the circumstances?

He would despise himself and not wish to live any longer.

Yes, but if he made his father and mother and brother and sister happy? Did not Christian want them to be happy?

Yes he did, but lying was another matter.

All men did that a little, and Christian should not make himself better than others.

All men liars! Christian had never believed that, and he himself had never lied.

That was because he had never needed to lie.

Why, that was dreadful! How could men live together if they did not speak the truth?

His sister said she could not explain that, but now she would go her way, and never wished to see again a brother who made her so unhappy.

Christian felt quite nervous by having so much attention concentrated on his person; he was not accustomed to people busying themselves about him, and this close dealing with his soul had disturbed his wonted equanimity. These people begged and implored him to do them a service; he could make them happy or miserable with a word—he was therefore a person of importance. This made him self-conscious, and he was seized with a desire to see the result of his intervention on their behalf. It was merely a matter of saying "yes" instead of "no," and after all what did it signify when all men were accustomed to change little words in case of need. Perhaps he would have fared better if he had done so before. His resolve was taken.

His father then entered and asked him if it was possible for a boy to collect such a stock of things?

Yes it was, if one did nothing else and was diligent.

His father could not believe it; he had never seen it and therefore found it incredible.

Christian repeated his affirmation. His father asked him to confess that he had stolen. Christian said "yes." His father, with the knife in his hand, asked whether he would confess to the bailiff. Christian promised solemnly to do so. His father cut the rope and they went together to the cottage. There sat the bailiff eating his porridge peacefully.

"Has he confessed?" he asked, letting his spoon rest.

"He has," said the father, to the great joy of those of the family who were present.

But the bailiff seemed to have made some miscalculation, for he was not glad.

"Well," he resumed, turning to Christian, "how did you manage it? I should like to know."

Christian, who would also have been pleased to hear how a single man sets about plundering a trader's boat, stood at first speechless, but as he began to think how he would act under the specified circumstances, his imagination came to his help. He went to the stand near the door, where the axes were kept, and took the largest gimlet he could see. Then he took down his father's great sheep-skin, threw it on the bed, and after he had taken his stand in the middle of the room, began thus. "There lies the boat at anchor" (be pointed to the bed) "and there lies the skipper asleep" (he indicated the sheep-skin).

"Wait! Let me think!" interrupted the bailiff, whose brain worked slowly.

But Christian continued. "Here I stand on the shore, watching the boat. Then I consider. There lies a boat and here am I. Probably there is something at the bottom of the boat."

Christian, who was not accustomed to lie, came to a stop, for his awakening conscience urged him to flight and freedom. Fortunately the bailiff utilised this pause to get his ideas into order.

"Let me see," he said. "There lies the skipper, and there lies the gimlet. What had you to do with the gimlet?"

Christian knew well, but that was, for the present, his secret. "I throw myself into the sea, my legs are entangled in the weeds, I wrench myself loose, swim to the anchor-rope, take the gimlet and sink the boat."

"That is too fast, too fast! Wait! Where were we?" said the bailiff. "We sank the boat."

He dipped the wooden spoon into the jug of milk, and continued.

"Well, and the cargo sank too?"

"Yes."

"That is remarkable. How did you get hold of it then?"

"I raised it," said Christian.

"He raised it. Quite right. Now I begin to see," said the bailiff, turning to Christian's father. "But," he resumed, after rubbing his nose with the spoon handle, "I do not understand why he sank the boat when he took the cargo."

"The skipper! The skipper!" broke in Christian's father, who was quite absorbed in the adventure.

"The skipper! Yes, that is quite right! He is a sharp youngster! It is a serious case, but finely managed."

Christian had had time to make his plan. He drew back to the door and asked, "Can I go now?"

The bailiff asked himself, "Can he go now?" Then he said, "Wait a moment! Did you not take up the skipper too?"

"No, I did not," said Christian, "but if the bailiff wishes it I will."

Then he disappeared through the door, with the sheep-skin on his shoulder and the gimlet in his hand, indicating his intention to save the skipper, and leaving those present to their reflections and discussions.

When Christian went out he went straight to the shore, reflecting how quickly he had become a liar and how comfortably lying helped one through the difficulties of life. Then he bored holes in all the boats except the largest fishing-boat, on which he hoisted sail and steered towards Trollhättor. There he put his stores on board till the sun rose, then hoisted sail again and held on in the sun's track.

Two years had passed. The old fisherman and his wife were dead. Their son Hans had taken over the farm and married a poor girl. Nothing had been heard of Christian, and at the division of the property he had been declared disinherited because he had left the country on account of a crime and nothing more had been heard of him. Hans' cottage stood on the shore of the fjord, just where it narrowed to a sound through which boats had to pass to reach the large fishing skerries. Exactly opposite the sound lay a little island about one acre in extent. It consisted mostly of hillocks, but in a hollow between them some earth had collected, covered with very good grass, and a score of birches had sprung up. Through his cottage windows Hans could see the island which was part of a neighbour's property.

One day during the spring thaw he sat and watched how the crows sailed on the pieces of ice in the sound; snow lay in patches on the banks, but there were glimpses of green in the clefts of the rocks. By chance he glanced over to the other shore and there perceived some movements going on which aroused his curiosity. Some workmen were bringing stones and timber already hewn and cut as if for building a cottage, but he could see no vessel which had conveyed the materials or the workmen. He could not rest till he had sent a servant over to his neighbour to ask what was going on. The messenger returned with the news that a stranger from Esthland had bought the island and was intending to build on it. This was all that Hans could discover at present. But not long after he discovered that the new-comer was his own brother, Christian, who had returned, accompanied by his wife whom he had married abroad. On mature consideration the risks for his freedom had not seemed great to him since no witnesses to hid adventurous plundering could be produced, and as regards the disappearance of the fishing-boat and the boring of holes in the others, there would only be a fine to pay, if his brother lodged a complaint against him.

Meanwhile the house grew higher and became such a stately building, with its outhouses, as to attract the attention of all who passed by, and to arouse the envy of Hans. One day he said to his wife, "I begin to think that this old house must be rebuilt."

"It is not long since that was done," she answered.

But Hans was wilful and had his own way. He was obliged to hire workmen who ate up his seed-corn and finished his winter stock of herrings.

"Pride comes before a fall," said people.

During the winter Hans sat in his large house and was half starved. In spring he had to sell a cow in order to buy seed.

Christian, on the other hand, lived comfortably in his roomy dwelling, though he possessed neither land, meadows, woods, fishing-grounds, cattle, nor yacht. Hans and he never met.

One evening the pastor, on his way from visiting a sick person, called in at Hans' house, and sat by the fire to warm himself. "I cannot understand how he has his train-oil factory far away in Esthland, and can sit here at home and manage it," said the pastor.

"Who?" asked Hans.

"He over there; Christian, your brother."

"Train-oil factory? He told my neighbour he was a rope-maker."

"Rope-maker? That is strange! Then one of us has heard wrong."

While they were discussing the matter, there was a knock at the door and the bailiff entered. He had been engaged in his business out of doors.

"It is quite incomprehensible," he said, "how one can sit here among the skerries and manage mines far away in Russia."

General commotion! Christian was a scoundrel! The pastor must go over and speak with him and the bailiff must find out how he supported himself.

The next day the pastor and the bailiff paid Christian a visit. They were received on the bridge and conducted into the house, which was handsomely furnished like that of a rich man, so that all questions as to Christian's means of subsistence were prevented. The floor was covered with smooth hewn planks, the fire-place was made of stone, and the walls were covered with hangings. Christian's wife was lively and pretty; her hair was black and hung over her eyes. She went round and poured Greek wine into their glasses while Christian related the moat extraordinary adventures of his travels which the pastor and the bailiff, under the influence of wine, found quite credible. This went on till late at night, and the pastor was carried down to the boat on a pair of oars, bestowing his blessing on tools and buildings and not least on Christian who had presented the church with a goblet of gilt silver. The bailiff, who had received a hunting-dog as a gift from Christian, was guided by it down to the boat where, placing his fingers on a tub of herrings, he took an oath that Christian was the most honourable man in the skerries.

Some time afterwards Christian came home, after an excursion among the skerries, in a great sailing boat rigged with two lateen sails which could hold straight against the wind and needed not to be taken down when he turned.

Hans now had no more peace. He must have lateen sails. His wife had been weaving linen during the whole winter for new shirts; Hans soon convinced her that the sails were more important. But he was also convinced, after bearing of the great reception which his brother had given to his guests, that a house-holder could not offer beer to his guests when a small-tenant offered wine. Still, wine was very dear, and he had a sharp struggle with himself as well as with his wife. He said they could economise with milk, to which he attached no special importance, and that he was quite willing to give up his own share of it. The second cow was sold.

Meanwhile wonderful reports began to go about and were repeated. Trollhättor was said to be haunted, and no one ventured to go there. Flames had been seen dancing over the sea. About that time there was a shipwreck, accompanied by the unusual circumstance that not one of the crew was saved. It seemed still more peculiar that Christian, shortly before the ship was driven on shore, had rented an inferior fishing ground among the outermost skerries, which had shallow banks and where no one wished to fish. He had been seen there carrying fishing-forks and lighting fires, but no one could understand why he went so far out with fishing-forks.

The reports increased and became threatening. But the pastor and the bailiff, who were regular guests at Christian's, took him vigorously under their protection, refuted the scandal, and thus the whole affair was forgotten.

When the spring came Hans had no seed-corn. He took no trouble about his patches of ground but let anything grow on them. He killed his own oxen for a baptism-feast which he held in March. No resource was now left to him but fishing. It was an insecure means of earning a living, almost like gambling. When he got nothing, he went hungry; when he had a good haul, he made a feast. His brother-in-law, who had a claim on his farm on account of his wife, caused him uneasiness also.

When the week of prayer before Easter arrived and the pastor came with the Holy Cross and the boys sang the litany round the fields in order to bless the seed sown, Hans was ashamed to acknowledge that his field had no seed sown in it. Then when only thistles appeared on it, people said he had betrayed the Cross of Christ.

The next year Hans had another son. Then he burnt up his last wood and sowed turnips in the ashes. But Christian sat on the shore exactly opposite, and saw how the beautiful island was changed to a bare skerry. He felt neither grief nor joy, but only found it instructive to watch the development of the affair.

In autumn Hans' turnip-crop failed, for the wood which had been a protection from the north wind was gone. One day, when their need was great and Hans had gone out fishing, his wife took a punt and rowed over the sound. Christian received her in a friendly way and bade her come into the guest-house where private conversations were generally held. She told him her great need and asked for help. Christian made no objection but gave help generously, including a cow, seed-corn, and so on. Hans' wife was moved, and confessed that her husband had not behaved well. Christian said he knew nothing about that and did not mix in other people's affairs. So they parted.

When she had gone, Christian said to his wife, "Olga, I have nothing more to do here. I have seen the punishment come without lifting my hand against my own flesh and blood. Hans is a beggar; in winter he will become a thief, since he must steal wood, after having burnt his trees. His children will become servants, if nothing worse. And that is right! They taught me to lie, and the representative of the law made me a thief. I was honest, but they would not let me be so. Now I could be so if I wished, for they have told me I can be an honorary magistrate, if I like to buy ground. But I will possess nothing of this earth for which men fight; I will not be respected by this society, who suspect that I am a scoundrel, and yet pardon me because I have a stone fire-place and drink wine. All my toils put together could not make me rich, you know, for one cannot become so by collecting skins and down. If I had lived three hundred years ago I would have been a pirate and my name would have been celebrated and cursed in the world. Then I would have staked my life and won my bread in honourable battle; now I am a wreck-plunderer and a corpse-robber, who enjoy the respect of everyone except my own—and thine, Olga. Let us leave this country which had no place for us when we were honest, but opened its doors when we were dishonest. Let us go where the earth has yet no owner, where the freeborn man can pasture his flocks, where the sky itself waters the grass, and the sun entices it to grow. Your eyes, Olga, ask me whether I shall not miss the old home where my childhood passed? I had no childhood; no one bade me welcome when I came, and no one says farewell when I go. When I saw you, Olga, my childhood began, and where you are, there is my home."

In the evening the Trollhättor was again haunted, and an incendiary set fire to Christian's house. By the light of the fire his largest boat was seen sailing out in an easterly direction. Christian sat at the helm, but his young wife sat in front by the main-sheet, keeping the look-out.

HIGHER AIMS

It was so cold in the little country church that the breath came like smoke from the mouths of the priest and the boys who sang in the choir. The congregation, who listened to the Mass standing, had been allowed to spread straw on the ground so that whenever they knelt at the ringing of the little bell, they should not be too chilled. To-day there were many people at Mass, because they were expecting an unaccustomed spectacle at the end of the service. The priest was going to admonish an ill-assorted couple, who would not keep the peace and could not divorce each other because no crime had been committed. Neither of them wished to leave their children and incur the disgrace of running away. The Mass was concluded and the litany, a "Miserere," sounded pathetically from the voices which trembled with cold. The sun shone redly through the frosted window-panes, and the burning wax candles gave no light at all, but looked merely like yellow blots over which the warmed air quivered.

"Agnus Dei, qui tollis peccata mundi," sang the priest; the boys answered "Miserere!" and the congregation joined in—deep clear men's voices and high soft women's voices—"Miserere—have mercy upon us!"

The last "Miserere" sounded like a cry of despair, for at the same moment the married pair stepped from the hidden place by the door, which had been appointed for them, and went up the central aisle to the altar. The man was tall, powerfully built, with a brown beard, and limped somewhat; the woman had a small, slender figure with pliant outlines and graceful movements. Her face was half hidden by a hood, so that one only saw a pair of pale blue eyes with a suffering expression, and the upper part of her white cheeks.

The priest said a low prayer and turned to the congregation. He was a young man, not yet thirty, whose fresh, good-natured face seemed to be out of keeping with his long robe and the solemn, severe words which he uttered. He had long ago received the confessions of each of the married pair, and only delivered his admonition at the bishop's command. The discordant couple had been to the bishop and had asked him to dissolve their marriage, but the latter had found no reason to grant their request since the canonical law and the Decretals only permitted divorce on account of sin, barrenness in certain cases, and the running away of husband or wife from hearth and home.

The priest began his admonishment in a dry, expressionless voice, as though he did not believe what he said. He declared that marriage had been established by God Himself, Who had created woman from the man's rib to be a help to him; but since the man was created first and the woman subsequently, the wife should be subject to the husband, and he should be her lord.

(Here the little hood made a movement as though the wearer wished to speak.)

The man on his side should treat his wife with respect because she was his honour, and by doing so he honoured himself in his wife. This was the teaching of St Paul in his Epistle to the Corinthians, chapter seven, verse four, on which passage the decree of Gratian was founded, declaring that the wife had not power over herself, but the husband.

(The little hooded figure shook from head to foot, and the man nodded approvingly at the priest's words. The priest, who now fastened his eyes on the woman, changed his tone.)

When the disciples came to Jesus and asked whether divorce was permissible for married people, be answered and said: "What God hath joined, let not man put asunder," and for this reason the Church did not allow the dissolution of marriage. The concessions made by earthly laws were only due to the wickedness of men and could not be approved by the Church.

Life was not a rose-garden, and we must not demand too much from it. The preacher himself was married (as at that time Catholic priests were allowed to be), he knew therefore how to judge in the matter; he knew that there must be give and take, if there was not to be quarrelling and strife. He had married this young couple and witnessed their first happiness; he had baptised their child and seen their love sanctified by parental joy. He reminded them of those unforgettable hours when life had given them its best and the future shone before them like a bright summer day. He adjured them by that recollection to reach each other their hands, and to forget all that had happened since the spirit of unrest had entered their hearts; he prayed them in the presence of that Christian congregation, to renew the tie which in their selfishness they had sought to dissolve.

There followed a moment of deep silence and expectation, while the congregation showed their impatience by pushing forward as far as the way they were packed together allowed. But the married pair remained motionless.

Then the priest seemed to become impatient, and in a voice trembling with annoyance and anger he again resumed. He spoke of the duties of parents towards their child, of God's wrath against an unforgiving temper, and said plainly that marriage was not meant to be merely a means of carnal indulgence or of increasing the population, but also—and he laid emphasis on this—of family education. He gave them till the following Sunday to think it over, and bade them depart in peace.

No sooner had he spoken the last word and made a gesture of dismissal with his hand, than the young wife turned and departed. Coldly and calmly she passed between the rows of the congregation, and disappeared through the great entrance. The man hesitated a moment, then he sought the smaller door at the end of the transept.

As the priest walked home with his wife, who had been present at Mass, she said to him in a gentle but reproachful tone: "Did you believe what you said?"

"You are my conscience, dear woman, and you know my thoughts; spare me therefore a little, for the spoken word smites like a scourge."

"Then let the scourge smite! You know by their confessions that the union of this married pair is no true marriage, you know that this woman is a martyr whose life can only be saved by her keeping away from this man; you know this, and yet you exhort her to go towards her destruction."

"The Church, you see, my friend, has higher aims than the well-being of ordinary people."

"I thought that the well-being of men, what you call their salvation, was the highest aim of the Church. What then is the Church's highest aim?"

"The increase of God's kingdom on earth," answered the priest after some reflection.

"Let us consider!" said his wife. "It is said that only the saved shall dwell in God's Kingdom. Then the Church is to save men."

"In the higher sense, yes!"

"In the higher sense; are there then two?"

"A little foolish woman can ask more questions than seven wise men can answer," said the priest, and pressed his wife's hand.

"Then it is a bad look-out for the wisdom of the wise, for what will they answer when an intelligent person asks—when all the intelligent people in the world come and ask?" continued the foolish little woman.

"They will answer that they do not know," whispered the priest.

"You ought to say that aloud, and should have said it to-day in the church. Your conscience is not pleased with you to-day."

"Then I will silence my dear conscience," said the priest, and kissed his wife, who was standing in the porch of their house.

"That you cannot," she answered, "as long as you love me; and certainly not in that way."

They stamped the snow from their feet and entered the little parsonage, where they were met by two small, healthy children, who wanted to kiss their father and mother. Not the least cause of the heartiness of their welcome was the good Sunday dinner which was cooking in the oven.

The priest took off his long clerical coat and put on one more like a layman's. In this, however, he never showed himself to any member of his congregation but only to his family and the old cook. The table was laid, the floor was clean and white, and the cut fir twigs smelt sweetly. The father said grace and they took their seats at the table as glad and as much at peace with the world and with each other as though a heart had never been broken for the sake of "higher aims."

The snow had melted and the earth reeked and fermented with creative power. The parsonage was situated on the unsightly plain in Uppland which is included in the ecclesiastical district of Rasbo. Wherever the eye looked there was only to be seen the stony ground, the clay soil, and some elder bushes which cowered like frightened hares before the never-ceasing wind. In the distance, on the horizon, were visible the tree-tops of the edge of a wood like the masts of a ship disappearing at sea. On the south side of the house the priest had planted some trees and hoed a little patch of ground where he cultivated flowers and vegetables, which in winter had to be covered with straw since they were not accustomed to this severe climate. A small stream which came from the woods in the north ran by the parsonage, and was large enough to row a punt on, if one kept exactly in the middle.

Dominus Peder in Rasbo had awakened at sunrise, kissed his wife and children, and gone to the church which lay a few stone's-throws from the parsonage. He had read the morning Mass, blessed the work of the day, and come home again beaming with joy and cheerfulness. The larks, which certainly did not understand the difference between beauty and ugliness, had sung over the stony fields as though they blessed the meagre crop. Water flowed murmuring in the ditches on whose edges gleamed yellow colt's-foot. The priest had come home, drunk his morning milk in the porch, and now he stood in his jerkin in the garden and released his flowers from their winter covering. He took a hoe and began to turn up the sleeping ground. The sun glowed; the work to which he was unaccustomed stirred his blood. He inhaled deep draughts of the strong spring air and felt as robust as though he had awakened to new life. His wife had opened the window-shutters on the sunny side of the house, and stood there dressing, while she watched her husband at work.

"That is better than sitting over books," he said.

"You ought to have been a peasant," she replied.

"I could not, my dear! Ah, how it does one's breast and back good! Why do people think God has given us two long arms if they are not to be used."

"Yes, one does not need them to read with."

"No! but to shovel snow, to hew wood, to dig the ground, to carry one's children, and to defend oneself—that's what they are for, and one is punished if one does not use them. We 'spiritual' men, we must not touch this sinful earth."

"Hush!" said his wife, and laid her finger on her mouth, "the children hear you."

Her husband took off his cap and wiped the perspiration from his brow.

"'In the sweat of thy brow thou shalt eat bread,' so it is written. Oh, how finely I sweat! That is something better than when anxiety at not being able to discover the sense of an obscure text makes one feel a cold sweat at the roots of one's hair, or when the spirits of doubt burn the goodness out of one's blood so that it creeps through the body like hot sand. Do you see how the flesh on my arm quivers for joy at being able to move? See how the blue veins swell like streamlets in spring when the ice melts, my chest feels so broad that the seams of the jerkin crack; that is really better— —"

"Hush!" said his wife, warning him again, and added, in order to divert the dangerous current of his talk, "You have released your flowers from their strait-waistcoats, but you have forgotten the poor animals who have stood all through the winter in their dark stable."

"That is true," said the priest, and put the hoe aside; "but then the children must come out and see."

He went at once to the cattle-house which stood at the back of the row of buildings of which the farm consisted; there he set free the two cows, opened the sheep and the calf sheds, then went up the little acclivity behind and opened the door of the pigsty. First came out one cow and stood in the door of the cow-house. The light seemed to dazzle her as she stretched out her neck and became aware of the sun; then she stepped carefully on the bridge and drew some deep breaths so that her stomach swelled; then she smelt the ground and as though seized by joyful recollections of the previous year, she erected her tail and danced up the little hill, leapt over stones and bushes and went off at full gallop. Then followed the other cow, the calves and sheep, and lastly the pigs. But behind them came the priest with a stick, for he had forgotten to shut the garden gate, and now there was a race, in which the boys eagerly joined, to drive the animals out of the enclosure. But when the old cook saw her master run up the hill in his jerkin she was anxious what people would say and rushed out from the kitchen door, while his wife stood on the steps and laughed merrily. But the young priest was so boisterous and joyful and delighted as a child at witnessing the delight of the creatures at the end of their winter imprisonment, that he forgot both congregation and bishop and ran out on to the high-road in order to drive the animals on to the fallow ground.

Then he heard his wife call his name, and when he turned round he saw a woman standing by her in the porch. Feeling ashamed and annoyed, he pulled his clothes straight, put his hair under his cap, and turned homewards assuming a solemn expression of face.

As he came nearer he recognised the little woman whom he had exhorted in the charge regarding discord in marriage. He perceived that she wished for a conversation, and asked her to come in, saying he would follow as soon as he had changed his coat.

In another coat and another mind he entered, after a time, the room where the unruly wife awaited him, and asked her business. She declared that she had come to an understanding with her husband that she should leave his house deliberately, since the Church would not grant a divorce in any other way. The priest was impatient and wished straightway to quote the Decretals and the Epistle to the Corinthians, when through the open window he heard the sound of a foot on the sanded garden-walk. He knew so well the light, soft step, and the crunching of the sand made an impression on his conscience.

"The act you contemplate, woman," he said, "is courageous, but it is nevertheless a crime."

"It is no crime; you only call it so," answered the woman decidedly, as though she had spent days and nights of despair in considering her action.

The priest was irritated, and sought in his mind for some cutting words when he heard again the sound of sharp crunching on the sand outside.

"You set a bad example to the congregation," he said.

"A worse one, if I remain," said the woman.

"You will be disinherited."

"I know."

"You will lose your reputation."

"I know that too, but I will bear it for I am innocent."

"But your child?"

"I will take it with me."

"What does your husband say to that? You have no claim on your child if you leave your home."

"Haven't I? Not on my own child? Then Solomon's wisdom itself is not sufficient to solve this tangled knot. But I will tear it in two, if I can make an end by doing so. I came to you to ask for light and you lead me into a dark passage, where you put out the light and go your way. One thing I know: where love ceases, there only shame and humiliation remain; I will not live in sin, therefore I break off."

Outside deep breaths, as of suppressed feelings, were heard. The priest struggled with himself, then he said: "As the servant of the Church, I have only to hold to the word of the Lord, and that is hard as a rock. As a man, I can only say what my heart suggests but what is perhaps sin, for the human heart is a frail thing. Go in peace, and put not asunder what God has joined."

"No, not what God has joined, but what our parents arranged. Have you not a word of comfort to say to me on the difficult path I have to tread?"

The priest shook his head negatively.

"May you not receive stones some day when you want bread," said the woman with an almost threatening look, and went out.

The priest threw off his coat again, sighed, and tried to drive away the uncomfortable feelings which the interview had caused. When he came out, he approached his wife with the remark that he was sincerely sorry for the poor woman.

"Why didn't you tell her so?" broke in his wife, who seemed to be well posted in the matter.

"There are things which one cannot say," answered her husband.

"To whom cannot one say them?"

"To whom? The Church, like the State, my friend, are Divine ideas, but being reduced to reality by weak men, are only imperfectly realised. Therefore one cannot confess before ordinary mortals that these arrangements are imperfect, for then they would begin to doubt their Divine origin."

"But if one, seeing their imperfection, should doubt of their Divine origin, and it should be shown, on examination, that they have no Divine origin?"

"I believe, by all the saints, that the devil of doubt reigns in the air of this time. Do you not know that the first questioner plunged mankind into damnation? Certainly it was not without reason that the Papal Legate in the recent Church Assembly called our land corrupted."

His wife looked at him as if she wanted to see how far he was in earnest, whereon her husband answered with a smile, which showed that he was jesting.

"You must not joke like that," said his wife. "I can so easily believe what you say. Besides, I never know when you are serious or making fun. You believe partly what you say, but partly not. You are so wavering, as though you yourself had been possessed by those spirits in the air of which you spoke."

In order not to proceed further in discussing a question which he preferred to leave untouched, the priest proposed to make a boat excursion to a pleasant spot which had the advantage of some leafy trees, and eat their midday meal there.

Presently he was plying his oars and the green punt shot over the smooth surface of the water, while the children tried to pull up the old reeds of the previous year, through whose dry leaves the spring wind whispered of resurrection from the winter's sleep. The priest had taken off his long coat and put on his jerkin, which he called his "old man." He pulled the oars strongly, like a practised rower, the whole half-mile to the birch-planted height, which lay like an island in the stony waste around. While his wife prepared the meal, he ran about with the children and plucked anemones and primroses. He taught them to shoot with bow and arrow, and cut willow-whistles for them. He climbed the trees, rolled on the grass like a boy, and let himself be driven like a horse with a bit in his mouth by the loudly laughing children. He grew ever more boisterous, and when the boys took the long coat which he had hung on a birch tree as a mark to shoot at, he began to laugh till he was purple in the face. But his wife looked carefully round on all sides to see whether anyone was watching them. "Ah! let me be at any rate a man in God's free world of nature," he said. And she had no objection to make.

The meal was laid on the grass, and the priest was so hungry that he forgot to say grace, which drew a remark from the children.

"Father does not say grace at table," they said.

"I see no table," he answered, and stuck his thumb in the butter. This delighted the children immensely.

"Keep your feet still under the table, Peter! Don't lay your legs on the table, Nils," he said, and the little ones laughed till they nearly choked. Never had they been so jolly; never had they seen their father so cheerful, and he had constantly to repeat his jests, which they heard at each repetition with the same delight.

But evening was coming on and they had to think of their return home. They packed up the things and got into the boat. They were still cheerful for a while, but soon the laughter grew silent and the children went to sleep on their mother's lap. The father sat quiet and serious, as one is after laughing much, and the nearer they approached the house the more silent he became. He tried at intervals to say something cheerful, but it sounded quite melancholy. The sun threw slanting rays over the huge fields; the wind had fallen; there reigned a depressing silence and deep stillness in all nature, only broken now and then by the lowing of cattle or the passionate crying of the cuckoo.

"Cuckoo in the north brings sorrow forth," said the priest, as though he would thereby give a long-sought expression to his melancholy.

"That is only true of the first time one hears it," said his wife, comforting him.

The roof of the cattle-shed was now visible, and behind it stood the church tower. They moored the punt by the bridge and the father took the two sleeping children and carried them into the house. Then he kissed his wife and thanked her for the pleasant day; he would now go to church, he said, and read vespers.

He took his book and went. When he came on the road the Angelus was ringing. He hastened his steps. From a good distance he saw people moving in the churchyard. Something unusual must be going on, as no one besides the sacristan generally attended vespers. He thought that someone had perhaps seen him on the island, and heard his conversation with his wife. He felt seriously anxious when he approached the church door, for there he perceived two horses with gorgeous trappings and an archdeacon with his retinue from Upsala, where the Archbishop lived. The archdeacon seemed to have been waiting, for he went immediately towards the priest and said that he wished to make a communication to him when vespers were over. Never had the priest read the evening service so fervently, and with deep anxiety he invoked the protection of all the saints against unknown dangers. He cast a glance now and then at the door, where he saw the archdeacon standing like an executioner waiting for his victim, and when he had said "Amen" he went with heavy steps to receive the blow, for now he was certain that a misfortune was impending.

"I did not wish to visit you in your house," began the Archbishop's messenger, "because my business is of such a nature that it demands a quiet place and the proximity of the holy things which strengthen our hearts. I have a message from the Church council to deliver which will deeply affect the intimacies of your private life."

Here he broke off, for he saw his victim's anxiety, and handed over a parchment which the young priest unrolled and read:

"Dilectis in Christo fratribus (dear brothers in Christ), Episcopus, Sabinensis, apostolicae sedis legatis (the Bishop of Sabina, Legate of the Roman Chair)— —"

His eyes flew over the crowded letters, till they stopped all at once at a line which seemed to be written in fire, for the young man's features became as pale as ashes.

The archdeacon seemed to feel sympathy with him and said: "It appears that the demands of the Church are severe: before the close of the year the marriages of all priests are to be dissolved, for a true servant of the Lord cannot live united to a wife without defiling the holy things which he handles, and his heart cannot be divided between Christ and a sinful descendant of the first woman."

"'What God hath joined, that shall not man put asunder,'" answered the priest as soon as he came to himself.

"That is only true for ordinary people; but when the higher aims of the Church of Christ demand it, then what would otherwise be wrong becomes lawful. And mark well the distinction—'*Man* shall not put asunder.' The saying, therefore, simply refers to man acting as the divider; but here God acts through His servant, and sunders what God has united, therefore it does not apply here."

"But God has ordained marriage Himself," objected the broken man.

"Just what I say, and therefore He has a right to dissolve it."

"But the Lord does not desire this sacrifice from his weak servant."

"The Lord commanded Abraham to sacrifice his son."

"But our hearts will break."

"Just so; hearts ought to break—that makes them more ardent in piety."

"I That can never be the wish of a loving God."

"The 'loving' God caused His own Son to be slain on the Cross. The world is no pleasure-garden, but merely vain and transient, and you may comfort yourself with the thought that the Decretals——"

"No, for God's sake, don't talk to me of Decretals! Archdeacon, in heaven's name give me a spark of hope; dip the tip of your finger in water and quench this fire of despair which you have kindled. Say that it is not possible; try to believe that it was only a proposal which was not adopted."

The archdeacon pointed to his seal and said, "Presentibus consulentibus et consentientibus (it is already decided and confirmed). And as regards the Decretals, my young friend, there are in them such treasures of wisdom that they may well serve to clear up a clouded mind, and if I want to give a good friend a piece of good advice, I say, 'Read the Decretals; read them early and late, and you will find that they make you feel calm and happy.'"

The unhappy priest thought of the stones which he had given on the morning of the same day to the despairing woman, and bowed his head to the blow.

"Therefore," concluded the archdeacon, "enjoy the short time left; the summer wind has blown, the flowers have sprung up in the field, and the voice of the turtle is heard in our land. On St Sylvester's Day *ultimo mensis Decembris* I come here again, and then must your house be swept and garnished, as though Christ the Lord was about to enter, under penalty of excommunication. Till then you can study the decree more closely. Farewell, and forget not to read the Decretals."

He mounted his white horse and rode away in order to reach the next parish before night and to spread grief and misery there, like the rider in the Apocalypse.

Dominus Peder in Rasbo was crushed. He did not venture to go home at once but rushed into the church, where he fell down by the altar. The doors of the gilded altar-triptych stood open, and the Saviour's progress to Calvary was illumined by the red rays of the evening sun. The priest was at this moment not the justiciary of a minatory and threatening Lord, but he lay like one of the chastised flock and prayed for mercy. He looked up to the image of Christ but found no sympathy there. The Saviour took His cup from the hand that offered it and emptied it to the dregs; He carried His cross on His mangled back up the steep hill where He was to be crucified, but over the Crucified heaven opened. There was then something over and beyond all these sorrows. The priest began to examine into the reasons of these great human sacrifices which were about to take place all over the country. The Church had seen how men began to doubt in the priest's right to be judge and executioner, for they had found their judges full of human weaknesses. Now the priests must show that for Christ's sake they could tear their hearts out of their breasts and lay them on the altar.

"But," continued his rebellious reason, "Christianity has done away with human sacrifices." He went on thinking, and the idea occurred to him that perhaps there was something underlying the old heathen sacrifices. Abraham was a heathen, for he did not know Christ, and he was ready to offer his son at God's command. Christ was sacrificed; all holy martyrs are sacrificed—why should he be spared? There was no reason why he should, and he had to acknowledge that if people were to continue to believe in his preaching they could also demand that, he should sacrifice his dearest himself, for he and his wife were one. He had to acknowledge this, and he felt a peculiar new enjoyment in the thought of the terrible sufferings which awaited him. Pride also came to his support and pointed to the martyr's crown which would elevate him above this congregation, on whom he was accustomed to look down from the high altar, but who had begun to raise their heads and defiantly threatened to storm this lofty position.

Strengthened and elevated by this thought, he rose and passed within the altar-rails. He was, in his own eyes, no more the crushed sinner, but the righteous man who deserved to stand by Christ's side for he had suffered as much as He. He looked proudly down on the praying-stools which in the twilight resembled penitents kneeling, and he hurled the denunciations of a prophet on their heads because they would not believe in his preaching. He tore his coat open and showed them his bleeding breast in which an empty gap showed that he had given God his heart. He bade those of little faith to put their hands in his side and let themselves be carried over by him. He felt himself grow during his suffering, and his over-excited imagination transported him into an ecstasy, so that the operations of thought seemed momentarily suspended and he believed that he was one with Christ. Further than that he could not go, and he collapsed like a sail which has been split by the wind, when the sexton came in to close the church.

On the way home be felt unhappy because his ecstasy was over, and he would have gladly returned to the church had not an indefinite something, which expressed itself as a faint sense of duty, summoned him home. The nearer he approached the more his religious emotions cooled, and the smaller therefore he felt himself. But when he entered the door, his wife received him with open arms, asking him uneasily why he had remained out so long; and when he felt the friendly glow of his hearth, and saw the children peacefully asleep with rosy cheeks, he realised the preciousness of what he had now to surrender. He felt all his young blood well up in his opened heart, and was conscious of the reawakening of the omnipotent force of first love which can bear everything. He swore never to leave the beloved of his heart, and the married pair felt themselves young again. They sat together till midnight talking of the future and how to escape the danger which threatened them.

The summer passed for the happy pair like a beautiful dream, during which they forgot the wakening which awaited them. Meanwhile the papal decree had become known to the congregation, who heard of it with a sort of malicious satisfaction—partly because they did not grudge their spiritual superiors a little purgatorial fire, and partly because they hoped to get their priests more cheaply when they had to live as celibates. Moreover, there were in the congregation a number of pious people who received whatever came from Bishop and Pope as though it came from heaven. They discussed the question thoroughly and adhered to the view that a priest's marriage was sinful. These pious people, who had expected to see the parsonage purified immediately after the promulgation of the decree, began to murmur when they saw that their pastor gave no signs whatever of intending to obey it. The murmuring grew in strength when the church-tower happened to be struck by lightning. This was followed by a failure in the harvest. The voices of complaint became louder and the pious party sent a deputation to the parsonage to declare that they did not intend to receive the sacrament at the hands of a priest who lived in sin. They demanded that he should separate from his wife, because any more children which might be born would be illegitimate, and they threatened to purify the parsonage with fire if it were not pure by the end of the year.

For a long time after that the pair were left in peace, but a marked change began to be observable in the priest. He went oftener into the church than he needed to, and remained there till late in the evening. He was reserved and cold towards his wife, and seemed as though he were nervous to meet her. He would take his children for hours on his lap and caress them without saying a word.

At Martinmas, in November, the archdeacon from the cathedral city came on a visit and had a long talk with the priest. That night the latter slept in the attic and continued to sleep there. His wife said nothing, but saw the course of events without the prospect of being able to alter anything. Her pride forbade her to make any advance, and as her husband began to take his meals alone, they met seldom. He was as pale as ashes, and his eyes were sunken in his head; he never ate in the evening, and slept on the bare ground under a sealskin rug.

Then came Christmas-time. Two days before Christmas the priest came into the house and sat by the oven. His wife was mending the children's clothes. For some time there was a dreadful silence; at last the man said: "The children must have something for Christmas; who will go to the town?"

"I will," answered his wife, "but I take the children with me. Do you agree?"

"I have prayed the Lord that this cup might pass from me, but He has not willed it, and I have answered, 'Let not my will but Thine be done!'"

"Are you sure that you know the Lord's will?" said his wife submissively.

"As sure as my soul lives!"

"I will go to-morrow to my father and mother, who are expecting me," said his wife in a sad but firm voice.

The priest stood up and went out hastily, as though he had heard his death-sentence. The evening sky was sparkling and cold, the stars glimmered in the blue-grey depths, and the boundless expanse of the snow-covered plain lay before the despairing wanderer, whose way seemed to point towards the lowest stars of the sky, which seemed as though they had risen out of the white earth. He wandered and wandered on and on; he felt like a tethered horse which runs but is pulled back by the rope whenever it thinks itself free. He passed by houses brightly lit up, and saw how people scoured and swept and baked and cooked in preparation for the approaching Christmas. Thoughts of his own approaching Christmas awoke in him. He imagined his house unheated, unlighted, without her, without the children. His feet were burning but his body felt freezing. He went on and on without knowing whither.

At last he stood before a house. The shutters were fastened, but a ray of light shone out and threw a yellow gleam upon the snow. He went nearer and put his eye to the chink. He saw into a room in which the seats and tables were covered with clothes—little children's shirts, stockings and coats. A large box stood open; on the cover of it hung a white dress whose graceful shape attracted his attention; it evidently belonged to a young woman, and on one shoulder was fastened a green garland. Was it a shroud or a bridal dress? He wondered with himself why corpses and brides were dressed in the same way. He saw a shadow thrown upon the wall—sometimes it was so large that it was broken by the ceiling and vanished in it; sometimes it crept down to the floor. At last it remained stationary on the upper part of the white dress. A small head wearing a cap was thrown into sharp relief against the bright background. This forehead, this nose, this mouth was familiar to him. Where was he? The shadow sank into the box, and into the light there came a face which could belong to no living person, so pale and unspeakably suffering did it appear. It looked him in the eyes so that they smarted, and he felt the tears roll down his cheeks and melt the snow on the window-ledge. The eyes of the face were so soft and pleading that he thought he saw St Katherine on the wheel, praying the Emperor Decius for mercy. Yes, that was she, and he was the Emperor. Should he grant her mercy? No; "give that which is Cæsar's unto Cæsar," says the Scripture. No mercy! But he could not endure these looks, if he was to continue to be strong; therefore he must go.

He now went into the garden, where the snow lay deep on his straw-covered flower-beds so that they looked like little children's graves. Who lay in them? His children. His happy, rosy-cheeked children, whom God had commanded him to sacrifice, as Abraham sacrificed Isaac. But Abraham escaped with only a fright. That must be a God of hell, Who could be so inhuman. It must be a bad God Who preached love to men but Himself behaved like an executioner. He would go at once and seek Him; seek Him in His own house, speak with Him, and demand an explanation.

He left the garden and waded through the snow-drifts till he reached a little fir tree by the wood-shed, and laid hold of it. That was a Christmas-tree like one the children would have danced round had they lived. Now he remembered that he wanted to seek the God Who had taken his children in order to bring him to account. The church was not far, but when he came to it it was closed. Then he became frantic. He scraped away the snow till he got hold of a large stone, and with that he began to hammer the door till the echoes from the church sounded like thunder, while he shouted loudly: "Come out, Moloch, child-devourer! I will split up your stomach! Come out, St Katharine and all saints and devils! You must fight with the Emperor Decius in Rasbo! Oho! You come from behind, legions of the abyss!" He turned round to the churchyard, and with the strength of a madman he broke down a young lime tree, and using it as a weapon he attacked the crowd of little grave-crosses which with out-stretched arms seemed to be marching against him. They did not flinch, and he mowed them down like Death with his scythe, not stopping till he had laid every one flat and the ground was covered with splinters of wood.

But his strength was not yet exhausted. Now he would plunder the corpses of his enemies and collect the dead and wounded. Load after load he carried to the wall of the church and piled them under a window. When he had finished he climbed on the pile, broke a pane of glass, and got into the church. The inside was quite lit up by the northern lights which had hitherto been hidden from him by the high roof of the church. He made a new raid on the threatening prayer-stools, which he battered into a heap of fragments. His eyes now rested on the high altar, where throned above the pictures of the Passion a figure sat on a cloud with the lightnings of the law in his hand. The priest crossed his arms and regarded defiantly the severe figure on the cloud. "Come down!" he shrieked. "Come down! We will wrestle together!" When he saw that his challenge was not accepted, he seized a block of wood and hurled it at his enemy. It crashed on a plaster ornament, which fell down and raised a cloud of dust.

He took another piece of wood and then another and hurled them with the mounting rage of disappointment. The clouds fell piece by piece, while he laughed loudly, the lightnings were torn out of the hand of the figure; at last the heavy piece of carving fell with a terrible crash on the altar and smashed the candlesticks in its fall.

But then the blasphemer was seized with a panic and sprang out of the window.

On the morning of the day before Christmas a parishioner had seen a strange sight by the hedge of the parsonage garden. A sledge came out of the enclosure containing a woman, two children, and a servant, and was driven westwards. At about a quarter of a mile distant it was followed by the priest running and calling out for the sledge to stop. But it had continued to proceed till it vanished round a bend of the high-road. Then the priest had fallen into a snow-drift, shaking his clenched fist against the sky. Later information came to the effect that the priest lay very ill with fever, and that the devil, in anger that he had not overcome the servant of the Lord in the battle waged for the dissolution of his marriage, had raged in the most terrible way in the church. But in order to enter it, and to exercise his power there, he had first broken down all the crosses in the churchyard. All this restored the priest's reputation and even gave him an appearance of sanctity, which especially pleased the pious party who had been the instigators of the purification of the parsonage.

The priest lay ill for three months and could not go out till April. He had become old. His face was full of angles, his eyes had lost their brightness, his mouth was half open, his back was bent. On the south side of the house he had a seat where he could sit in the warmth of the sun, buried in dreams of the past which hardly possessed any reality for him, especially as he had received no news from those whom he had once called his own.

Then the month of May returned with flowers and the song of birds. The priest went into his garden and saw how it was overgrown with weeds;

his precious flowers were killed by the frost because no one had seen to their being covered, and they now lay mouldering like rags upon the earth. It never occurred to him for a moment to break up the soil round the flower-beds or to do anything else of the kind, since he had no one for whom to work and there would be no tending hand to protect the young growths. He stood by the fence and looked out over the landscape. The plain stretched away in the sunlight and the little brook rippled merrily and invited his eyes to follow the little wavelets, which danced by and aroused his longing to follow them southwards, where they met the river. He unmoored his boat, sat in it without touching the rudder, and let it drift with the stream, gliding on thus for about two hours.

Suddenly he was aware of the fresh scent of budding birches and spring flowers. He looked round; the plain had ceased, and he found himself at the beginning of the little birch wood. Memories of the previous year rose in him; bright, phantom-like images hovered above the primroses and anemones. He stepped on shore and went up the hill. Here they had eaten their lunch; here on this branch hung the coat at which the boys had shot with their bows. He saw the hole which he had bored in the birch tree to draw off the sap, which the little ones had drunk. The willow still bore scars from the knife with which he had cut arrows. He found an arrow in the grass; how they had hunted for it—the best he had ever cut, which flew above the top of the highest birch tree! He hunted in the grass and bushes like a pointer; he upturned the stones, bent back the branches, raised up the previous year's grass, scratched away the leaves. What he sought for exactly he did not know, but he wished to find something which might remind him of her. Finally he stood by a hawthorn bush; there hung a small fragment of a piece of red woollen cloth on a thorn. It was set in motion by the wind and fluttered like a pretty butterfly between the white hawthorn blossoms—a butterfly pierced by a needle. Then there came a second gust of wind and turned it round, so that it looked like a bleeding heart—a heart that was torn from a victim's breast and hung on a tree. He took it down from the bush, held it to his mouth, breathed on it, kissed it, and hid it in his hand. Here she had played "soldiers" with the children, and they had trodden on her dress.

He lay down on the grass and wept; he called her name and the children's. So long did he weep that he fell asleep from exhaustion.

When he awoke he remained lying as he was for a time and looked with half-closed eyes over the grass meadow. His eyes fell on a large willow bush whose yellow tassels hung like golden ears of corn in the sunshine. His tears had calmed him and produced a certain peace in his mind; sorrow and joy had ceased, and his soul felt in equipoise. The reason that his eye rested on the willow bush was that it was directly in his line of sight. A gentle wind swayed the branches lightly, and their movement seemed to soothe his tear-reddened eyes. Suddenly the branches of the bush stopped swaying with a jerk; there was a rustling, and a hand bent the boughs to one side; a sunlit female figure appeared framed in the gold of the willow tassels and the green of the tender leafage.

He still lay a while watching the beautiful sight, as when one looks at a picture. Then his eyes met hers, which looked out of the bush like two stars; they kindled, as it were, flame in his expiring spirit. His body rose from the earth and his feet carried him forward; he stretched out his arms, and the next moment he felt a small warm creature nestle on his stony bosom, which was again filled with the breath of life, and a long kiss melted the ice which had so long held his spirit imprisoned.

Eight days later the archdeacon came on a visit to the parsonage at Rasbo. He found the priest happy and contented. The archdeacon had a commission which made him somewhat embarrassed, and he found he had to express himself suitably. Rumours, he said, had been heard in the congregation which had reached to the Archbishop's chair. One should not certainly believe all reports, but the mere fact of a report arising was itself half a proof. The priest, to speak plainly, was said to be having assignations with a woman. The Archbishop was fully aware of the storm which the Papal Bull regarding priests' marriages had occasioned. The Holy Father himself had recognised the cruelty involved in the new law, and had therefore thought it advisable through a special "licentia occulta" (a secret permission) to make the lives of the clergy less difficult. Woman, it must be admitted, was the presiding genius of home life.

Here the current of his eloquence stopped, and in a low, scarcely audible voice the messenger of Christ whispered the secret sanction.

The priest answered, "Then the Church does not allow a priest to have a wife, but only a mistress?"

"Don't use such strong words! We call it a 'housekeeper.'"

"Well then," said the priest, "if I take my wife as a housekeeper, the Church has nothing against it?"

"No! No! Take any other, but not her. The aims of the Church! Remember!"

"The *higher* aims of the Church," you said. "So it was to annul the right of inheritance and to get possession of land that the Church insisted on divorce, not in order to check sin! You consider therefore the unlawful seizure of other people's property as 'higher aims.' Very well then! I will have nothing to do with the Church. Excommunicate me, and I will consider it an honour to be excluded from the fellowship of the noble Church. Depose me from my office, and I will be so far away before you have been able to write your proclamation that you will never be able to find a trace of me. Greet the Holy Father from me, archdeacon, and tell him that I do not accept his dirty offer. Greet him and say that the gods whom our forefathers worshipped above the clouds and in the sun were greater and much purer than these Roman and Semitic cattle-drivers whom you have foisted upon us. Greet him and say that you have met a man who will devote his whole future life to converting Christians to heathenism, and that a day will come when the new heathen will undertake crusades against the vicegerent of Christ and His followers who wish to introduce the custom of sacrificing men alive, whereas the heathen contented themselves with killing them. And now, archdeacon, take your Decretals and go away before I flog you soundly. You have nearly killed two people here with your invisible 'higher aims,' and the whole land calls down a curse on you. Go with my curse; break your legs on the high-road; die in a ditch; may the lightning strike you and robbers plunder you; may the ghosts of your dead relations haunt you; may incendiaries set your house on fire—for I excommunicate you from the society of all honourable men, as I excommunicate myself from the Holy Church! Get out!" The archdeacon did not remain long in the parsonage; nor did the priest, for his wife and children were waiting for him by the hill planted with birch trees on the way to the wood on the border of Vestmanland, where he was going to plant a settlement.

PAUL AND PETER

Christmas Eve lay bitterly cold and silent as death over Stockholm; everything living seemed to be frozen; there was not a breath of wind and the stars seemed to be flickering like little flames in order to keep themselves alive. A lonely watchman ran up and down the street to keep his feet from freezing, and the beams cracked in the old wooden houses.

In the dwelling of the tradesman Paul Hörning in the Drachenturm Street his wife had already risen. She did not venture to light a candle or to kindle a fire, for the early-morning bell in the city church had not sounded, but she expected it every moment for she knew it was about four o'clock. The whole household was going to early Christmas Mass at Spånga, and must have something warm first. She searched for her Sunday clothes which she had laid on a chair, and dressed herself in the dark as well as she could; but as she found waiting in the darkness wearisome, she lit a horn-lantern, trusting that the watchman would respect the peace of Christmas and not raise an alarm, and then she stole around the low little rooms.

Her husband was still half asleep and little Sven was far away in the land of dreams, although he lay with his head on a wooden horse and a feather ball in his hand. Karin, who had been confirmed in the autumn, was still asleep behind the curtain, and had hung her new velvet jacket and her necklace of Bohemian crystal on the bedpost. The Christmas-tree, with its red apples and Spanish nuts, threw long, jagged shadows over everything and made it look ghostly in the faint light.

The mother went out into the kitchen and awoke Lisa in the box-room, who started up with tempestuous hurry and lit the candle in the iron candlestick; she was not anxious about the light being seen, for she was good friends with the night-watchman Truls, and besides, the kitchen lay at the back of the house. Then the mother knocked on the ceiling with the broom handle for Olle the shop-boy, who slept in the attic, and he knocked three times with his shoes in reply.

After that she went again into the bedroom and sewed a hook and eye firmly on her husband's starched and smoothly ironed shirt with its stiff collar. Then she took little Sven's red stockings out of the great oak chest, and held them against the light, and busied herself with one or two other small matters. Finally she awoke Karin, who put two small freshly bathed feet in straw shoes and began to dress behind the curtain, for there was very little room.

Sven awoke of his own accord; his cheek had a red mark where it had rested on the wooden horse, and he began at once to throw his feather ball, which flew over the curtain and hit his father on the nose, awaking him, so that he grunted a greeting of "Happy Christmas!" from his huge bed which was built like a small house. Sven wanted to run behind the curtain and see his sister's Christmas presents, but she screamed and said he mustn't for she was just washing herself.

Then the city church bell began to ring for early Mass; all murmured a blessing. Mother set the chandelier in the large room; Sven came there with nothing but his shirt on and sat under the Christmas-tree trying to make himself and others believe that he was in a wood. Then be gnawed the back side of an apple so that it should not be seen, but the apple revolved on the thread by which it was suspended; mother came and said she would slap him if he did not go at once and dress himself. Lisa lit the fire on the hearth so that the flame roared up the chimney, and placed the milk kettle on it; mother spread a cloth over the great table in the sitting-room and set out the plates, putting the brightly polished silver jug in father's place, then she cut slices of bread and butter and ham, for one must have something before going out so early.

Olle had already been a good time on his legs and gone into the stable; he had awakened Jöns the stable-man and curry-combed the chestnut horses. The sledge was drawn out of the coach-house and the rugs were dusted; soon the sledge stood in the street and Olle kindled the torches, which lit up the walls of the house like a conflagration. Jöns cracked the whip as a signal that the horses had been harnessed, and the latter snorted and scraped the ground with their hoofs to show their impatience.

In the house they were searching for their upper garments—furs and hoods, cloth-shoes and muffs; Karin, who was ready first, went down and offered Olle and Jöns a drink of hot ale. When Paul Hörning was dressed he took a glass of French mulled wine. His wife locked everything up and came after him with Sven and Lisa, and so they were all safe and sound outside in the street.

The sledge was a strong one, as roomy as a barge, and had three seats; on the first sat Paul and his wife and little Sven, on the second, Karin and Olle, and on the last Lisa and Jöns with the torches. Paul got in last for he had to see whether the horses were properly shod, and whether the harness was straight; then he got in, and his weight made the body of the sledge creak. He took the reins, asked once more if anything had been forgotten, cracked the whip, nodded to the windows of his old wooden house, and then they were off! First to the Great Market, where they met other good friends among the horse-possessing citizens of Stockholm. There they sat already in their sledges—stout brewers and thin bakers, and the whole market-place was lighted up by their smoking torches. The horses' bells tinkled, and now the whole procession began to move down the slope and out of the northern city gate.

"I am wondering how Brother Peter will receive us this year," said Paul to his wife when they had settled down for the drive.

"Why so?" she asked, somewhat uneasily.

"Oh, of course, he has no reason, but I think I annoyed him too much last year about the salt, and since then, according to my observation, he has been rather reserved."

"Well, if it were so he would not show it, I think; you two do not meet so often, and although you are not real brothers, you have always considered yourselves such."

"But Mats is very resentful, and if there were the slightest difficulty, it would stop all prospect of a match between him and Karin. We will see! We will see!"

Little Sven sat below in the straw and held the ends of the reins in the belief that he was driving. Olle, the shop-boy, tried to talk sentimentally to Karin, but her thoughts were somewhere else and she did not answer; Lisa, however, let Jöns hide her hand in his great glove, and sometimes she helped him to hold the torch when his hand froze.

Outside the city they passed under the ridge of the Brunkeberg, over the moor, and on the high-road towards Upsala. Soon between the fir trees the lights of the church of Solna were visible, glimmering in the dark winter morning. Here Paul parted from his fellow-townsmen, who remained there because they wished to go by the Westeras road to Spånga. Soon little Sven was wondering at the great Christmas-trees on both sides of the road, which were lit up at intervals by the torches and immediately hidden in darkness again. He thought he saw kobolds standing behind the tree-trunks with their red caps and beckoning, but his father told him they were only the red reflections of the torches flying and running, for his father was an intelligent townsman who no longer believed in kobolds.

Sven thought that the great Christmas-trees were running along by the side of the sledge, and that the stars were dancing over their tops, but his mother told him that God dwelt in the stars and that they were dancing to-day for joy that the Christ-Child was born, and Sven quite understood that.

Now they passed over a bridge which rumbled under the horses' hoofs, the wood became clearer, the plain expanded before them, and little hills planted with birch copses appeared here and there. Presently a light shone from a cottage window and they saw someone carrying a torch towards it. In the distance above the plain appeared the morning-star, shining very large and bright. Olle the shop-boy told Karin that it was the star which had led the shepherds to Bethlehem, but Karin knew that herself, for in a large town one knows everything, and Olle was from the country.

The road took one more turn, and through the long boughs of the leafless lime trees the church could be seen with all its windows brightly lit up. By the church wall the torches had been thrown into a great blazing pile by which the coachmen warmed themselves after they had taken the horses to the stable. Paul cracked his whip, swept past the bonfire in a stately curve, and made his chestnut horses curvet before the admiring peasants.

At the church door they met Peter and his wife and his tall son Mats. They embraced each other, wished each other a happy Christmas, and asked after one another's health. After they had talked for a while, the bells rang a second time, and then they entered the church. There it was as cold as though one were sitting in the sea, but they did not feel it for they froze in good company, and for the rest they had the preaching and the singing to keep them warm. The young ones had so much to look at; they went about and greeted each other, and were never tired of staring at the great chandeliers.

When at last the early service was at an end and they came out again on the hill, the stars shone no longer, but in the east the sky was reddish yellow like a ripe apple. Then they trotted quickly to Peter's house. It was a large one with back premises, guest-rooms, and bed-rooms on the attic floor. By one of the railing posts was tied an unthreshed sheaf of corn on which the sparrows had already settled and were keeping Christmas; at the house door stood two fir trees which sparkled in the frost.

Peter placed himself there and bid his foster-brother and his belongings welcome; then they entered the house and took off their furs. Peter's wife, who had gone before them, stood by the fire and heated ale, his son Mats helped Karin to take off her fur, and Sven was already rolling in the Christmas straw which covered the ground to the depth of half a yard. Paul and his wife were led to the sofa and took their place under the blue and red hangings on which were depicted Christ's entry into Jerusalem, and the Three Wise Men, while Peter sat down in a high armchair.

The long table presented a stately appearance, for there was not a handbreadth which was not covered with a dish or a bowl. The table was laid for the whole of Christmas, and all the eatables in the house were set out on it: a whole boar's head grinned on a red painted wooden plate, surrounded by brawns, tongues, joints and briskets; there were butter-dishes and loaves, cakes and wafers; jugs of sweet-scented juniper-wood filled with foaming Christmas beer. The red light of early morning shone on the little green, hoar-frosted windows, and it looked as though it were summer outside; but within, the great fire on the hearth spread a splendid warmth. Peter took his pocket-knife and cut slices of bread, spreading butter thickly upon them with his thumb, and invited his guests to do the same. When the hot ale had been drunk, the taciturn host opened the conversation, for Paul was a little embarrassed how to begin.

"Did you have a good journey from the town or not?"

"Splendid!" answered Paul. "The chestnuts ran along like lightning!"

But Peter did not like the town horses and always ignored them when Paul made an ostentatious allusion to them.

"Is corn selling well this Christmas?" he continued.

"The price is low, for those confounded Livlanders had a fine harvest."

"And you grudge it them! Don't curse the harvest, brother! You don't know what you may come to. The more one curses the she-goat, the more it prospers!"

"But I must live too!"

"Plough, rake and sow, and you will reap."

"Ah, the old story!"

"Yes, the old story! The priest reads in the church and prays God for a good harvest, and the tradesman in the town grumbles when God gives it. To the deuce with such people who wish to thrive on the needs of others!"

Paul was about to answer but now the two wives intervened and begged them for heaven's sake to keep the Christmas peace.

The two opponents were silent, and threw angry glances at each other; but Mats and Karin drank at the same corner of the table out of the same jug, and the two old women looked at each other with a meaning smile.

"Pass me the salt," said Peter, and stretched out his arm.

Mats passed his father the salt, but spilt some on the table-cloth.

"Be careful with God's gift," said Peter. "Salt is very dear."

Paul felt the thrust, but kept silence. The women gave a new turn to the conversation, and a storm was averted. When Paul and Peter had finished eating they went out in order to get fresh air and to inspect the fields and animals. They began by visiting the cattle-stall.

"What will you give me for this?" asked Peter, pulling the calf's tail.

"When he is an ox, and you bring him to the town in the spring, I will tell you."

"There is nothing to prevent me, but I won't bring my ox to town."

"We shall see," said Paul.

"What shall we see?" asked Peter, and looked at him with his head on one side. "I understand your dodges well enough, but though a sow may get her snout through a paling it does not follow that she will get her body through too."

"We shall see! We shall see!"

Peter would not ask any more.

They went on and came to the stable. "What will you give me for this?" asked Peter, lifting the black stallion's hind leg. "It is ten and a quarter to its backbone."

"My left chestnut is eleven, and the right is ten and a half," said Paul.

Peter did not apparently hear this, but opened the stallion's mouth in order to show its fine teeth.

"That horse is like a sheep," said Paul. "You try that with the chestnut, and you will never hear a cuckoo again."

"Everyone speaks to his like," said the muller, and talked to the sow.

The conversation would not flow. They looked at the sheep and the pigs, but either Paul's interest seemed forced, or the proximity of the chestnut horses, who were in the stable close by, had a disturbing effect; at any rate, they were out in the fresh air again and took a walk in the fields. The snow prevented Peter going into effusive details, but he pointed out where he had done his autumn sowing, where the spring sowing would take place, and where the fallow ground lay. Then they had to inspect the stacks of wood and straw to see whether they were dry or damp, to find out whether the bees were frozen in their hives, and whether it was too hot for the geese in their house.

By this time it was nearly noon and the bell rang for High Mass. Then they went again into the church and had a midday nap and went home to eat. They ate for three hours and then enjoyed the twilight. The elder men sat in their chairs and nodded; their wives sat by the fire which blazed so brightly that it dispelled the darkness, and chatted about weaving and baking. Mats and Karin had seated themselves on a box and whispered about their affairs. Olle the shop-boy had his arm round Lisa and Jöns his round the maid-servant; they sat on the ground and guessed riddles whose solution caused little Sven great difficulty. But the glow on the hearth became more subdued, the talk became more intermittent; the elders snored, the women nodded, and Mats and Karin nestled closer together; the lads and maid-servants became still, and soon an afternoon sleep prevailed throughout the house.

Peter's wife awoke first, and it was quite dark; she blew up the fire on the hearth and made a blaze. The men woke up gradually and there was a stir in the room. The youths, girls, and women sat down in the Christmas straw round the fire to crack nuts and tell stories. Paul fetched a bottle of Spanish wine, with which to make himself and Peter jolly while they talked and played cards to while away the long winter evening. When they had filled their glasses and drunk to each other, Peter remarking that the wine was too sweet, Paul boldly seized the threads of the conversation in order to bring them into order and began: "Now, Brother Peter, if you want us to talk about a matter you know of, draw out the cork and let it flow."

"That's all right," said Peter, "but I have always thought when the right Abraham comes, Sarah dances. Good! What will you give your boy?"

"Just as much as you give your girl."

Peter scratched his head. "It depend! what sort of year this is. The dowry runs into money, and if I have a bad year, there will be no money, and one does not know how it will go, for the snow came in autumn on the seed when the fields were wet."

"Just the same with me," said Paid. "We will let it stand over till the autumn, and if we can both produce the same amount we will let the organ blow, as the verger says, and if fortune is kind the ox will calve as well as the cow."

"Very well! And so the matter remains: the boy and the girl must wait till the corn is in the ear."

Then they began to drink; but the younger ones had pushed away the straw and sat in a circle to "hunt the slipper." Paul and Peter sat for a while looking on at the game; at last Paul felt exhilarated by drinking, and felt strongly tempted to start a more lively conversation. He knew very well how to do so.

"Well, Peter," he resumed, "are you coming to the city this winter?"

Peter showed his teeth like an ill-tempered dog, looked at Paul to see if he meant it seriously, and said:

"N-no! I don't think I shall!"

"Still as prejudiced against the town as ten years ago? What! Can you not bear to look at it through seven palings?"

"I wouldn't have it as a gift, if you threw it at me! I don't need it at all, but it can't live without me."

"So you say!"

"So I say! I have meat and hay, beer and bread, fuel and timber, house and clothing; what do I want with you then? I build my house, I plough my field, I cut my wood; my old woman spins my yarn, weaves my coat, bakes my bread, and brews my beer. What do you do? You tax my crop; you impose tolls on my wood; you empty my granary. You settle down on a stone as bald as the palm of my hand; you neither sow nor plough, but you reap and gather into barns; you eat my bread and drink my beer; you burn my wood and spin my wool; you sit there like a lazy monk and take tithe, and what do you give me for it?"

"Listen! Listen!" stammered Paul. "Don't you get my salt?"

"Your salt! You make no salt; and if you had not grabbed at it, so that we needed you as a middleman, you could not grind us down. And your sugar? I do not need your sugar, I have my bees!"

"Don't you get my iron?"

"Your iron! Where do you dig that up? In the gutters? What!"

"Don't you get my wine?"

"Where do you plant it? On the roofs?"

"Don't you get my silver and my gold?"

"What should I do with them, even if you had any? Can I make a knife, a plough, a spade, a brush, or a winnowing-fan out of them? No, I won't have any of it. All your business is useless, and if there were not so many fools to buy your stuff, you would starve. Remember, if all the 'louts of peasants,' as you call them, recovered their reason, so that they did not take the trouble to change their crops for your rubbish, what would you eat then? What?"

"Eat? One does not live in order to eat."

"No, but one lives by eating. And those who live by cheating others can also keep race-courses and dancing-houses where one learns such fine things; they can print books where one can read that all which the idle do is well done, and that it is honourable to steal if one only takes a sword in one's hand, sticks a rag on a pole, marches into a foreign land and says 'Now there is war!'"

"You always bring up the old race-course again. We paid the King ourselves for it, so that we might keep it in peace."

"Paid it yourselves! Yes, how did the matter go? When it was made, it was said that the town should pay for it; then you complained, and said they were such bad times, for the peasants would not buy your goods. And what did you do then? You put up the price of salt. Yes, I remember it well, and you shall be paid back for it. And so the peasant had to pay for the race-course and all your other tomfoolery, for that you must have, for you have jammed yourselves together like bees in a hive and see neither the sun nor the moon."

Peter's intoxication began to gain the upper hand, and he had an inner vision of the hated chestnut horses as embodying the showiness of the town.

"And though you have not so much grass as can grow on my chin, yet you can support two chestnuts. What do they eat? Sugar and salt? What! Raisins and almonds perhaps? And what do your chestnuts do? Do they plough; do they draw logs of wood or a load? No, they keep clear of all that. I know well what they draw, but that I don't say; but I know well that the streets there are not longer than my turnipfield. Yes, that is what they can do, the lazy beggars. Deuce take me if I don't have a turn at being idle. Listen, mother, do you want to be idle, then we will get a pair of red chestnuts with Cordova-leather trappings and silver knobs on the harness. Come, mother, we will be idle, then we can drive in a blue painted sledge with the servants behind, put our feet in foot-warmers of otter-skin, and then we can sleep out the morning with a velvet cap on our head, and drink Spanish wine sugared. Eh, mother, come! We will be lazy too!"

Paul began to get angry. "I believe the Spanish wine has got into your head, although you neither planted it nor pressed the grapes," he said.

Peter felt that he had been insulted, but he was too befogged to understand it at once. "The wine, you say, and I think you shrug your shoulders. Remember he who has got a loose tongue must cover his back. One fellow may sneeze into a silk handkerchief and another may throw it on the ground, but both can eat out of the same trough. What are you talking about wine for? Have I looked into *your* mouth? Do you think I have nothing of my own to drink? May the devil take your wine! Come out in the courtyard and I'll make you feel something!"

Peter threw away the rest of his wine and got up in order to go out. Paul was held back by the women who begged him for Christ's sake not to go. Peter would cool down, they said, and the Christmas peace should not be disturbed. Peter was envious and did not like anyone to "boss" him. Paul at first wished to return to the town at once, but gradually he let himself be smoothed down and took part in the game, while Peter worked off his rage outside. It was not long before there was a knock at the window and a little while after at the door. When they opened it, Peter entered it, wearing a sheep-skin, and hobbled about like a goat, so that the straw on the floor was all sent flying and the others jumped up on seats and tables. Their merriment soon became uproarious; they ate and drank without any more quarrelling till night-time, and then they went to sleep.

When the Christmas festivities were over, Paul returned home with his family, and Karin and Mats were an engaged couple. It was arranged that the wedding should take place in the following autumn, if the harvest and trade were good. So the new year began with hope for the younger ones and renewed effort on the part of their elders.

When the first snow fell on the following November, Peter harnessed his black stallion to the sledge and took Mats with him, in order to drive to the town and talk about the wedding. The harvest had been better than they had dared to expect, and Peter could give a fair sum as a dowry. There was a splendid surface on the high-road for the sledge, and Peter was in a good humour, although he could not dispel a certain uneasiness at again coming to the town, where he had not been for ten years, and where he had met with a number of misadventures which made him dislike the town-dwellers. For the same reason Mats had never been able to make a journey to the town till now, when he found himself on the way to a place full of wonderful things, the description of which, with embellishments which he had heard from returning peasants, had sounded to him like fairy-tales.

They went along briskly, for the stallion was a good sledge-trotter, and it was not long before the North Bridge rumbled under the horse's hoofs. Mats was quite stupefied at the wonders which he saw—houses as large as mountains and standing so closely together!

"See!" he said, "what good neighbours they can be to each other, and we in the country can hardly keep the peace at a quarter of a mile's distance. And so many churches! How religious they are! And the town hall right in the middle where one can get justice the whole day long!"

Peter made a grimace, and answered nothing.

They came to the tollgate, which was politely opened and closed again without their having to get down from the sledge. Mats thought that that was a good custom for he knew what a trouble it was to open a heavy gate, but Peter cracked his whip so that the horse began to run, for he wanted to enter the town as a person of importance. But they heard a cry behind them, and two of the city guards ran at them with lowered halberds, while a third seized the horse by the bridle and brought the sledge to a standstill, "Are you trying to bolt, you d——d lout of a peasant!" shouted the gate-keeper, coming up.

"Bolt?" asked Peter humbly, beginning to remember his former misadventure in the city.

"Hold your mouth and come!"

The black stallion was led back to the toll-house, where the travellers had to wait for half an hour, while the sledge was searched and their names were written down. They were at last liberated with an order to proceed at a walking pace.

When they reached the Smiths' Street, the sledge-runners began to knock against the stones, for the snow had been cleared away. The horse exerted himself and pulled with all his strength, but they only advanced step by step and could not understand why it was so difficult. Peter struck the horse, but it was already doing its best with its loins strained, and its hoofs struck sparks from the stones of the street. Mats simply sat there staring up at the high houses and marvelling at the wonderful things which hung outside them: here were horseshoes and carriage-wheels; there were fiddles, lutes, trumpets; there clothes, sets of harness, and guns. The baker had hung up a large B-shaped biscuit, the carpenter a table, the butcher a sheep! "They must have very little room inside," he remarked to his father, when at the same moment a snow-ball flung from behind struck off his cap. Peter and Mats turned round and saw that the whole back part of the sledge was packed with boys. "Be off with you!" said Peter.

The boys put out their tongues at him. Then Peter raised his whip and struck at the mass of them, but was so unfortunate in his stroke that the whiplash caught the eye of a baker's boy, who uttered a frightful yell and dropped a basket of loaves which he was carrying. At the same time people came running together and an angry blacksmith mounted on the sledge and gave Peter such a blow on his mouth and nose that he saw sparks. "Are you striking the boy, you stupid ox of a peasant?" he cried.

Mats was about to intervene and to throw himself on the smith, when the crowd of people joined in. The fighting waxed furious, and Peter and Mats had been soundly thrashed when the guards came up and finished the matter by taking down the names of the two disturbers of the peace and summoning them to the town hall.

"This is worse than being in an enemy's country," said Peter, "for here one cannot defend oneself."

"What have you got to do here then, ox-driver?" said the smith.

"I have to bring you food, or you would be hungry," said Peter.

"Listen to the clodhopper," said the smith. "They have no manners, these mud-larks, when they come among people, but they will learn some, you bet!"

The black stallion was set free and had to draw the sledge with the back part full of boys, who had settled upon it like crows upon a piece of carrion, up the street.

"That is very strange," said Mats, "that these devils of boys have a right to ride free."

"That is municipal law, you see," answered Peter.

"Yes, but the civil law doesn't allow it."

"The civil law is not in force here," said his father.

Now they had reached the great market-place. Here Peter stopped and got down. The boys were discontented because they could not go farther, but Peter asked humbly for consideration.

He looked for something he could tie his horse to till he had found his brother, whose address he had forgotten. He saw a stake with rings attached to it standing in the middle of the market-place, which seemed suitable, and to this he tied his horse, while the onlookers grinned and made jests at his expense which he did not understand. Then he turned to the one who looked most sensible and asked for the house of his brother Paul. There were fifty Pauls all tradesmen and just as many Peters, so that he could get no exact information. Peter and Mats now felt hungry and proceeded to look for a tavern. Paul, they thought, was such an important tradesman that they would be sure to be able to find him some time.

As they walked away they came to the ironmarket. Horses were being sold there, and there was much to look at.

"See!" said Mats, "there are the chestnuts, I declare!"

Peter stared with wide-open eyes. There were really Brother Paul's chestnuts which had turned up again. A sinful longing to possess them awoke in him, and he inquired the price. It was very high, but would not his heart exult if he could drive with them to his brother's door and call to the coachman, "Unharness the chestnuts! Take the chestnuts to the stable! Give the chestnuts their oats"? And how the peasants would stare when he came home with them, and had the black stallion tied behind as an extra horse!

So he gave the seller earnest-money, and said he would fetch the horses later in the day. The bargain was sealed with some food and beer in the iron-market tavern, and Peter found out from the merchants where his foster-brother lived—in the seventh cross-street on the left hand. Peter and Mats began to count the streets, but did not get more than half-way to the seventh, for they had to stand and stare at the quantities of strange things exposed in the shops for sale. Besides, the street was very narrow so that they collided with foot-passengers and carriages, and received thumps before and behind. They got quite out of their reckoning and had to return to the iron-market and begin counting again.

After they had repeated this process more than once, they were tired and thirsty and went into a tavern. But when they came out again, they did not know their right from their left; the afternoon had come on and it was twilight. Then Peter remembered the black stallion which had nothing to eat or drink, and after asking their way several times they reached the Great Market. But instead of the black stallion and the sledge, which had disappeared, they found two of the city police waiting for them. These, after writing down their names, took them by the collar and marched them to the lock-up for the night. Peter tried to defend his freedom from what he called violence, but was immediately knocked down and had his hands tied behind him. He demanded an explanation, but that, he was told, would be given him next day, and in such a manner that he would remember it.

The two prisoners were taken to a long vaulted room under the town hall, which was filled with men of every age and class. A horn lantern threw a feeble light over the prisoners, who sat or lay on benches placed along the wall. Never had Peter and Mats seen men of such an appearance or in such a condition. Their clothes were in rags, their faces savage and their gestures wild, but however wretched and humiliated they might be, they had one common feeling—contempt and dislike for the new-comers. They accosted them in an insulting way and made fools of them as soon as they opened their mouths.

"Take a chair and sit down, peasants!" cried a half-drunken porter as they entered.

Mats, suspecting no evil, thanked him and looked about for the chair which was not there. All those present burst into laughter.

The porter, who because of his physical strength and active tongue had chosen himself as chief speaker, proceeded to examine the new arrivals in a magisterial tone.

"What have you done, peasants, that you have the honour of entering this high-born society?"

"We have done nothing at all," answered Mats, in spite of his father's beckoning him to be silent.

"Just like ourselves," answered the porter; "but if we do nothing that is our right, but you, peasants, are born to work. But you don't work. In spring you scratch the crust of the earth a little, and throw some handfuls of com on it, and then you go about and watch it growing. Do you call that working? Then comes summer and you dance the hay in, and drink over it. Then it is autumn and you go to bed and sleep through the winter. Is that work? You ought to sit in the fortress Elfsborg and hew stones, then you would know what work is."

"If you envy us, then go and be a peasant," answered Peter.

"I a peasant? Oh fie! I would rather be an executioner or a night-watchman! Envious, do you say? Am I envious? Will anyone assert that? Do you know why I sit here? You should know, for you will think twice afterwards before calling me envious."

"Well, tell us!" answered Peter. "Tell us!"

"Shall I tell you, peasant—you with your corn-sacks? It is your fault, I tell you, that I sit here. Do you know Paul Hörning? No, you don't. Well, he was a corn-merchant, and since he let himself be persuaded in the spring by a scoundrelly peasant that there would be a bad harvest, he bought all the corn he could get hold of and had his granaries full. But it turned out that the peasant had lied; there was a good harvest and corn fell in price. Paul Hörning got into a mess; he had to sell his chestnut horses and dismiss all his servants. So I lost my place and loafed about, and now I sit here. Such are the tricks of these rogues of peasants!"

Mats stared, and Peter was very sad.

"I am sorry to hear what you say," answered Peter, "but it is not my fault that God gives the harvest."

"Don't talk about it, for I won't listen. Isn't it your fault that you won't be content with what you have but sow such a hellish lot of corn that the corn-merchant is ruined. You should be content with what you have, then others too might be able to live. I really feel inclined to thrash you a little when I think well over it. Shall I thrash him a little? What do you others say?"

The onlookers were of different opinions. A shoemaker's apprentice opposed the idea, for he had discovered that bread was cheaper when the peasants had much corn. A German shop-boy, who served in a general store shop, had no objection to a good harvest for then the peasants were more willing to buy stores. An organ-grinder, with a monkey perched on his shoulder, had no objection to the peasant being thrashed, for the peasants never had money with them, but he had nothing to say against a good harvest for then the market was full. A butcher said that Peter should be beaten black and blue, for when the farmers had a good crop it sent up the price of oxen. A wood dealer said he didn't want anyone to be beaten, but remarked that if the peasants had a good harvest they became proud and would not chop wood; but when there was a bad harvest, wood could be had for nothing, and one could eat flesh every day. This last remark made the shoemaker change his mind, for he had noticed that the price of leather fell when the farmer had to kill his cattle.

The porter, whom all these contradictory opinions could bring to no conclusion, was himself of opinion that Peter must be thrashed on principle, and that thrashings never did any harm. But when he approached Peter with unsteady steps, in order to carry out his purpose, he was immediately knocked down by Mats, who intervened. Since the porter was only too glad to rest his heavy head, he used the opportunity and remained lying there; and as no one else wished to do the same there followed a silence in the room.

Peter and Mats drew off their furs, and made a bed of them as well as they could for the night's sleep.

"It is just as if we had fallen among the Danes," said Peter when they had crept under the furs to sleep; "and yet they call themselves our countrymen! But to-morrow, I hope, we shall get justice."

Mats, for his part, had lost all hope that they would obtain justice from the city law, and was very depressed. He said, as usual, his evening prayer aloud. He prayed for his father, mother and fiancée; he asked God to shield them from fire and danger; he asked for a good harvest and good government; and finally prayed God to protect all men good and bad alike.

This unusual sight again evoked various opinions among the spectators. The butcher thought it was hypocrisy to pray for one's enemies, since it was one's duty to defend oneself against them. The shoemaker scented mischief in the prayer for harvest and said it was equivalent to praying for the downfall of one's fellowmen, as had just appeared in the case of Paul Hörning. The organ-grinder thought one ought not to pray for the Government, for the Government built prisons, and prisons were expensive and unnecessary; he could not understand what people wanted with them, since freedom was a man's inalienable right and highest, good. He and his monkey had never had a fixed abode, and they were quite happy if they could only be free. The wood-dealer did not like people praying God to interfere with fires and such-like, the fire-brigade were well paid for that; he said the peasants had only mentioned the subject because he was a wood-dealer and liked to have his wood burning on people's hearths. He also thought that the Government was quite unnecessary; if people would not look after themselves and their families, let them be left alone—the Government should only mix in foreign affairs.

Peter and Mats, who were tired by their exertions and troubles, fell asleep during the talk, and presently all the others followed their example. Soon only the sighing and snoring of the sleepers were audible. But the monkey could not sleep; he jumped up and ransacked all the pockets he could reach in order to find a crust of bread, but did not succeed; he rustled through the straw and pulled the hair of one of the sleepers, who cried out and went to sleep again; he climbed up to the lantern and extinguished it; then he became frightened at the darkness, felt for the organ and began to turn the handle, but received a cuff from the organ-grinder. Them a new idea seemed to come into his head; he looked for the drunken porter and found him, bit all the buttons off his coat, and threw them high in the air, so that they fell down again on the sleeping man. When the uneasiness which this produced in the sleeper had subsided, he began to tear the porter's coat into small strips, which he then twisted up into a ball. When this was done, he fell on his knees, and folded his hands, as he had seen his master do after a bad day. Then he placed the ball under his head and fell asleep.

When Peter and Mats awoke next morning the warder stood ready to take them into court. When they came before the magistrate he appeared to be in a great hurry and contented himself with reading the verdict on the "peasant Peter from Spånga" who was accused (1) of trying to elude the observation of the guard at the city gate; (2) of having beaten a boy; (3) of having tied his horse to the pillory in the Great Market. The sentence was that he should be fined. Peter asked permission to speak; the judge bade him be silent, for one was not allowed to speak in one's own cause. On Peter's inquiring who was to speak then, he was conducted out of court and had to pay the fine.

"That is the city law, you see," he said to Mats when they had come outside and obtained possession of their horse and sledge again. "Now we will sit up and drive home. We can send for the chestnuts another time, and Brother Paul can wait, and you too, Mats. A year passes quickly when one is young."

Mats did not like this, and asked leave at any rate to go and greet Karin, but Peter was inexorable, and they started for home. When they had got outside the city gate, Peter turned round and put out his tongue. "Well," he said, "if I ever set foot inside there again, the deuce take me! If you townspeople want anything from me, you can come and look for it!"

As they approached Solna, Peter suddenly started and looked away over his horse's ears. "Deuce take me," he said, "do I see ghosts in broad daylight? Look, Mats, can you see anything red over there?"

Mats did see something red, and Peter whipped up the black stallion. They soon came up to the horse-dealer with the two chestnuts, who had long waited for his customer in vain.

Now the bargain was concluded, and proud as the merchant Paul himself, Peter yoked the chestnuts to the sledge, tied the black stallion behind, and drove fast home. When they reached the farm Peter's wife stood in the vestibule, and thought her brother-in-law bad come from the town. When she saw how the matter stood she became sad and said, "Didn't I say that people get proud simply by going to town."

But Peter was so glad to be home again that he did not listen to his wife, and the chestnuts added to his cheerfulness. The thought that Paul had received a lesson put him in quite a good humour, so that he hummed to himself as he led the chestnuts to the stable.

But Mats was not cheerful, for a year was a long time to look forward to, and he knew already that when milk begins to curdle it soon becomes sour.

This Christmas Paul did not come to Spånga, although Peter had promised to fetch him in the sledge with the chestnuts; he said he had too much to look after.

Spring came and the young corn looked hopeful; but in autumn it rained at the critical time and continued to rain day and night, so that the corn fermented in the ear, and the straw rotted, and there was a bad harvest. Peter was obliged to send the chestnuts to the town and sell them. But that did not help much, for as he had no straw he had to try to sell some of his cattle also. His servant, however, brought the oxen back, for the price offered in the town was so low, because all the farmers' harvests had failed and they had also sent in their oxen to be sold. Peter became uneasy, for he expected Paul to come at Michaelmas. He therefore had the oxen taken over to Dannemora, where they would, as he knew, fetch a higher price.

Michaelmas Day had come. Peter's wife was standing by the fire cooking sausages; Mats was in the room above putting on his best clothes. Peter ran about restlessly, and went sometimes out on the road to see whether his servant were not returning with the money, for to-day Paul would come, and he must lay the sum for his daughter's dowry on the table. Peter, who had experienced many mishaps during the past year, had a dim foreboding that this day would not be a cheerful one.

It was a sunny autumn morning, but the north wind was blowing so that it was partly cold and partly warm, and Peter felt the same in his own person. It was quite certain that his servant had sold the oxen, but he was uneasy at his not arriving. He longed for Paul to come so that the business might be finished, but at the same time feared his coming. So he walked up and down the road—looked northwards for his servant and southwards for Paul; at one time he had the north wind at his back, then in his face, and so with the sun. At last he heard in the distance a sound like carriage wheels rumbling over a bridge, and then there was silence; he stood quite still and stared in the direction of the town; he shaded his eyes and looked. What he feared came. It was inevitable. He saw two reddish horse heads appear, and behind them what looked like a wobbling house-roof. It was Paul who came in a covered carriage drawn by two chestnuts. He had a carriage, thanks to the bad harvest, and the scarcity of corn had helped him to recover the horses.

Peter wanted to go into the house and hide his head behind the chimney corner, but Paul and his womenfolk had caught sight of him and waved their pocket-handkerchiefs. Peter lifted his cap and pretended that the sun dazzled him; Mats came running out and opened the carriage door. Peter's wife stood as usual in the doorway and began to curtsy when she saw the carriage. Then they entered the house, where the meal was ready for the guests. Paul talked about the state of the roads and the last war; Peter discussed the question of the church-tithe. Peter's wife was busy with the sausages and the mutton, Mats was absorbed in conversation with Karin, and no one mentioned the bad harvests, the chestnuts, or any topic that might disturb the peace.

When they had eaten, Peter and Paul went out. But Peter had no desire to show the cattle-stalls and the granary, and Paul took care not to mention the chestnuts. But at last the other subject, which Peter had most feared, turned up. Paul began, "Now, Peter, are you ready to settle the matter? The children are pining for each other, and time is passing."

Peter looked northwards, as though he wished to fetch the answer from thence. "You will stay over dinner," he said, "and we can talk about the matter then."

"Perhaps you are not ready with the money?" said Paul. "That would be a pity, for I have just now several offers."

"I not ready with the money? Ha! ha! My money does not melt so quickly as other folks', and although I do not get rich by bad harvests, yet I am not poor."

"Perhaps, brother, then you will be so good as to lay the money on the table; then I will go home to dinner."

Peter felt uneasy. "No! after dinner," he answered quietly. "After waiting so long you can wait a little longer, and I don't think it will hurt you."

At that moment they heard the sound of horses' hoofs. Peter started and looked down the road. There came his servant riding, without the oxen; therefore he must have the money. He assumed a more confident tone and continued, "But, brother, if you happen to be in embarrassment, I will produce the money at once!"

The servant came nearer, but he was not alone. Beside him rode an armed man who held the end of a cord, the other end of which bound the servant's hands. The horses splashed on through the mud and stood still. Peter was dumb.

"Halt," cried the bailiff's man. "You, Farmer Peter, have sent your servant to carry on illegal traffic. What have you to say?"

"Where are my oxen?" asked Peter.

"Forfeited," answered the bailiff's man.

"Next time, four hundred marks' fine; the third time, death."

"Who has made that law?"

"The King."

"Formerly we made the laws ourselves. When did we give up the right to do so?"

"When the council and the nobles did."

"They never proposed to give the King permission to steal our oxen."

"Weigh your words, Peter, for God's sake!" said Paul warningly.

"Hold your tongue!" answered Peter. "It is you and fellows like you who sit in the town and pass laws for their own profit. So it goes on! The King needs money for races and triumphal arches; he takes it out of the merchant's purse, and the merchant takes it out of the farmer's. Who prevents me selling where I choose?"

"The law," answered the bailiff's man. "But don't stand scolding there, farmer. Untie your servant's hands and give my horses something to eat."

Peter was beside himself. He ran like a madman into the house. Then he took a poker and swept the bowls and dishes from the table on to the ground; he broke the windows, drove all those present out of the room, smashed the seats and tables, and roared all the time till he foamed at the mouth; he chewed pieces of glass, broke tin plates in two, and trampled on butter-dishes and jugs. Then he stood in the doorway and shouted, "Out, you hellish thieves! Once right was law in the world, now wrong is law. Thieves make laws for honest folk, and now they steal legally. You, petty merchant, don't work a bit, but eat my bread; don't you know that you ought to pay for it? I have a right to flog you, for you are one of my dependents! And you, underling of your thievish masters—you, King's official! What do *you* do for your bread? You make entries in a book—you all do that; you note everything down. If I drive on the road, if I lie down, if I tie my horse, if I defend my property, if I flog a scoundrel, you make a note of it, and I must pay for everything. Holy Virgin and all the saints, preserve my understanding! And now take your chestnuts and your women away, Paul; and if you appear on my land again, remember what you have brought me to. Buy a son-in-law in the town for yourself; there you will make a good bargain if you can pass her off on one of your friends. You may have got me down on my knees, but I am not rotting, as the old woman said, when she fell into the churchyard. To that I say Amen! and praise and thank God for good and evil!" But Paul and his womenfolk had already gone to the stable and harnessed the horses. As they drove through the gate Paul said, "Poor Peter has gone mad!"

But Paul and Peter never met again. Mats never got Karin, and there was no help for it; it was so fated and no one could alter it.

A FUNERAL

The cooper sat with the barber in the inn at Engsund and played a harmless game of lansquenet for a barrel of beer. It was one o'clock in the afternoon of a snowy November day. Hie tavern was quite empty, for most people were still at work. The flames burned brightly in the clay fire-place which stood on four wooden feet in a corner, and looked like a coffin; the fir twigs on the ground smelt pleasantly; the well-panelled walls kept out all draughts and looked warm; the bull-finch in his cage twittered now and then, and looked out of the window, but he had to put his head on one side to see if it was fine. But it was snowing outside. The innkeeper sat behind his counter and reckoned up chalk-strokes on a black slate; now and then he interjected a humorous remark or a bright idea which seemed to please the other two.

Then the great bell in the church began to toll with a dull and heavy sound, in keeping with the November day.

"What the devil is that cursed ringing for?" said the cooper, who felt too comfortable in life to enjoy being reminded of death.

"Another funeral," answered the innkeeper. "There is never anything else."

"Why the deuce do people want to have such a fuss made about them after they are dead," said the barber. "Trump that, Master Cooper!"

"So I did," said the cooper, and pocketed the trick in his leather apron.

Down the sloping road which led to the Nicholai Gate, a funeral procession wended its way. There was a simple, roughly planed coffin, thinly coated with black paint so that the knots in the wood showed through. A single wreath of whortleberries lay on the coffin lid. The undertaker's men who carried the bier looked indifferent and almost humiliated because they were carrying a bier without a cover and fringes.

Behind the coffin walked three women—the dead man's mother and her two daughters; they looked crushed with grief. When the funeral reached the gate of the churchyard, the priest met it and shook hands with the mourners; then the service began in the presence of some old women and apprentices who had joined the procession.

"I see now—it is the clerk, Hans Schönschreiber," said the innkeeper, who had gone to the window, from which he could overlook the churchyard.

"And none of his fellow-clerks follow him to the grave," said the cooper. "A bad lot, these clerks!"

"I know the poor fellow," said the barber. "He lived like a church mouse and died of hunger."

"And a little of pride," added the innkeeper.

"Not so little though," the cooper corrected him. "I knew his father; he was a clerk too. See now! these fellows who go in for reading and writing die before their time. They go without dinner and beg if necessary in order to look fine gentlemen; and yet a clerk is only a servant and can never be his own master, for only the King is his own master in this life."

"And why should it be more gentleman-like to write?" asked the barber. "Isn't it perhaps just as difficult to cut a courtier's and to make him look smart, or to let someone's blood when he is in danger of his life?"

"I would like to see the clerk who would take less than ten years to make a big beer barrel," said the cooper. "Why, one knows the fellows require two years to draw up their petitions and such-like."

"And what is the good of it all?" asked the innkeeper. "Can I scribble such letters as they do, but don't I keep my accounts all right? See here I draw a crucifix on the slate—that means the sexton; here I scribble the figure of a barrel—that stands for the cooper; then in a twinkling, however many strokes I have to make, I know exactly how much each has drunk."

"Yes, but no one else except yourself can read it, Mr Innkeeper," objected a young man who had hitherto sat silent in a corner.

"That is the best of it," answered the innkeeper, "that no one can poke his nose into my accounts, and therefore I am just as good a clerk as anyone."

The cooper and the barber grinned approval.

"I knew the dead man's father," resumed the innkeeper. "He was a clerk too! And when he died I had to rub out many chalk-strokes which made up his account, for he wanted to be a fine gentleman, you see. All the inheritance he left to the son, who now lies with his nose pointing upwards, was a mother and two sisters. The young fellow wanted to be a tradesman in order to get food for four months, but his mother would not consent; she said it was a shame to step downward when one was above. And heavens, how the poor young fellow had to write! I know exactly what went on. The three women lived in one room and he in a rat-hole. All he could scrape together he had to give them; and when he came from work to eat his dinner, they deafened him with complaints. There was no butter on the bread, no sugar on the cakes; the elder sister wanted to have a new dress, and the younger a new mantle. Then he had to write through the whole night, and how he wrote! At last when his breast-bone stuck out like a hook and his face was as yellow as a leather strap, one day he felt tired; he came to me and borrowed a bottle of brandy. He was melancholy but also angry, for the elder sister had said she wanted a velvet jacket such as she had seen in the German shop, and his mother said ladies of their class could not do with less. The young fellow worked and slaved, but not with the same zest as formerly. And fancy! when he came here and took a glass to ease his chest, his conscience reproached him so much that he really believed he was stealing. And he had other troubles, the poor young fellow. A wooer came after the younger sister—a young pewterer from Peter Apollo Street. But the sister said 'No!' and so did the mother, for he was only a pewterer. Had he been a clerk, she would have said 'Yes' and persuaded him that she loved him, and it is likely that she would really have done so, for such is love!"

All laughed except the young man, who struck in, "Well, innkeeper, but he loved her, although she was so poor, and he was well off; that proves that love can be sincere, doesn't it?"

"Pooh!" said the innkeeper, who did not wish to be interrupted. "But something else happened, and that finished him. He went and fell in love. His mother and sister had not counted on that, but it was the law of nature. And when he came and said that he thought of marrying, do you know what they said?—'Have you the means to?' And the youth, who was a little simple, considered and discovered that he had not means to establish a new family since he had one already, and so he did not marry; but he got engaged. And then there was a lot of trouble! His mother would not receive his fiancée, because her father could not write, and especially because she herself had been a dress-maker. It was still worse when the young man went in the evenings to her, and would not stay at home. A fine to-do there was! But still he went on working for his mother and sisters, and I know that in the evening he sat and wrote by his fiancée's side, while she sewed, only to save time and to be able to be near her. But his mother and sisters believed evil of the pair, and showed it too. It was one Sunday about dinner-time; he told me himself the young fellow, when he came here to get something for his chest, for now he coughed terribly. He had gone out with his fiancée to Brunkeberg, and as they were coming home over the North Bridge, whom did they meet but his mother and sisters? His fiancée wanted to turn back, but he held her arm firmly and drew her forward. But his mother remained standing by the bridge railings and looked into the water; the elder sister spat before her, and did the same, but the younger—she was a beauty! She stood still and stared at the young woman's woollen mantle and laughed, for she had one of English cloth—and just because of that, her brother's fiancée had to wear wool. Fancy the impudent hussy!"

"That was simply want of sense in the child," said the young man.

"Want of sense!" exclaimed the cooper indignantly. "Want of sense!" But he could not say any more.

The innkeeper took no notice of the interruption and continued: "It was a Christmas Eve, the last Christmas Eve on which he was alive. He came to me as usual to get something for his chest, which was very bad. 'A Merry Christmas, Hans!' I said. I sat where I am sitting now, and he sat just where you are sitting, young sir. 'Are you bad?' I asked. 'Yes,' he answered, 'and your slate is full.' 'It doesn't matter,' I answered, 'we can write down the rest in the great book up there. A glass of hot Schnapps does one good on Christmas Eve.' He was coughing terribly, and so he took a drink. Then his tongue was loosened. He said how miserable and forlorn he felt this evening. He had just left his home. The Christmas table was laid. His mother and sisters were soft and mild, as one usually is on such an evening. They said nothing, they did not reproach him, but when he took his coat and was about to go out, his mother wept and said it was the first Christmas Eve that her son was absent. But do you think that she had so much heart as to say 'Go to her, bring her here, and let us be at peace like friends.' No! she only thought of herself, and so he went with an aching heart. Poor fellow! But hear what followed. Then he came to his fiancée. She was glad and happy to have him, and now she saw that he loved her better than anything else on earth. But the young man, whose heart was torn in two, was not so cheerful as she wished him to be, and then she was vexed with him, a little only of course. Then they talked about marriage, but he could not agree with her. No, he had duties towards his father's widow. But she quoted the priest who had said a man should leave father and mother and remain with his wife. He asked whether he had not left his mother and home this evening with a bleeding heart in order to be with her. She replied that she had already noticed, when he came, that he was depressed because he was going to spend the evening with her. He answered it was not that which depressed him, but his having to leave his old mother on Christmas Eve. Then she objected that he could not deny he had been depressed when he came to her—and so they went on arguing, you can imagine how!"

The cooper nodded intelligently.

"Well, it was a pleasant Christmas for him. Enough! The young fellow was torn in two, piece by piece; he never married. But now he lies at rest, if the coffin nails hold; but it was a sad business for him, poor devil, even if he was a fool. And God bless his soul! Hans Schönschreiber, if you have no greater list of debts than you had with me, they are easily settled!"

So saying, the innkeeper took his black slate from the counter, and with his elbow rubbed out a whole row of chalk-strokes which had been made under a hieroglyph which looked like a pen in an inkpot.

"See," said the barber, who had been looking through the window to hide his red eyes, "see, there she is!"

Outside in the churchyard the funeral service was at an end; the priest had pressed the hands of the mourners and was about to go; the sexton plied his spade in order to fill up the grave again, as a woman dressed in black pressed through the crowd, fell on her knees by the edge of the grave, and offered a silent prayer. Then she let fall a wreath of white roses into the grave, and a faint sobbing and whispering was audible as the rose leaves fell apart on the black coffin lid. Then she stood up to go, erect and proud, but did not at first notice in the crowd that her dead lover's mother was regarding her with wild and angry looks as though she saw her worst enemy, who had robbed her of her dearest. Then they stood for a moment opposite one another, revengeful and ready for battle; but suddenly their features assumed a milder expression, their pale faces twitched, and they fell in each other's arms and wept. They held each other in a long, convulsive embrace, and then departed side by side.

The innkeeper wept like a child without attempting to hide his emotion, the barber pressed his face against the window, and the cooper took the cards out of his pocket as though to arrange them; but the young man, his head propped in his hands, had placed himself against the wall in order to have a support, for he wept so that his whole body shook and his legs trembled.

The innkeeper first broke the silence. "Who will now help the poor family? The pewterer would be accepted now, were he to make another proposal."

"How do you know that, innkeeper?" asked the young man, much moved, as he stepped into the centre of the room.

"Well, I heard it yesterday when I was up there helping at the preparations for the funeral. But the pewterer will not have her now, as she would not have him then."

"Yes he will, innkeeper!" said the young man. "He will have her though she were ever so selfish and bad-tempered, poor, and wretched, for such is love!"

So saying, he left the astonished innkeeper and his friends.

"Deuce take me—that was he himself!" said the barber.

"Things do not always end so happily," remarked the cooper.

"How about the clerk?" objected the barber. "No, they did not end well with him, but with the others, you know. They had, as it were, more right to live than he, the young one; for they were alive first, and he who first comes to the mill, grinds his corn first."

"The young fellow was stupid, that was the whole trouble," said the barber.

"Yes, yes," concluded the innkeeper. "He certainly was stupid, but it was fine of him anyhow."

In that they were all agreed.

THE LAST SHOT

On one of the last days of October in the year 1648 there prevailed much bustle and activity in the streets of the little town Lindau on the Lake of Constance. This Swabian Venice, which lies on Three Island close to the Bavarian coast, had long been besieged by the Swedish Field-marshal Wrangel, who during the last years of the war had been operating in conjunction with the French and had pitched his fortified camp on the hill in the village of Eschach.

The negotiations for peace, which had already lasted four years, had not yet resulted in any cessation of hostilities, only lately Königsmarck had stormed Prague. But this event had accelerated the negotiations in Osnabrück and Münster, and rumours of a coming peace had reached Swabia. Lindau had for many months been suffering all the terrors of a siege. During the last days the bombardment from Eschach had ceased, and the burgomaster, who had returned from a secret visit to Bregenz, had on the afternoon of the above-mentioned day betaken himself to the inn "Zur Krone," for the town hall had been demolished. He hoped to meet there some acquaintance who was not on duty on the fortifications. In the rooms of the inn he had met no one, and feeling rather depressed, he went out on the terrace to cast a look over the town and to see what the Swedes were doing in their camp on the opposite shore.

The Lake of Constance lay there in unruffled calm, and the snowy summit of the lofty Santis was reflected in it; the edge of the Black Forest loomed like an evening cloud, misty-blue in the west, and in the south the Rhine rushed between the Vorarlberg and the Rhetic Alps till its yellow waters flowed into the blue-green depths of the lake. However, the burgomaster had no eye for this kind of beauty, for during the last eight days he had been half starved, and for more than a month he had been suffering and fighting. He only looked down on the road along the shore where good-natured Bavarians mingled with quarrelsome Würtembergers and lively Badenese; he could also see people flocking to the Franciscan church to take the sacrament. Down by the shore he noticed a group of men, who stared out on the lake where some barrels drifted, borne along by the light current; they were busily occupied in drawing these to land with boat-hooks and ropes.

"What have you there, men?" called the burgomaster down from the terrace.

"That is a present from the honest Swiss in St Gall," answered a voice.

"Probably wine or must which has lain in the lake and waited for the west wind in order to float down here from Romanshorn," said another voice.

The burgomaster drew back from the terrace and went down to the dining-room of the inn to sit there and wait for the result of this haul of flotsam and jetsam. The apparently immovable face of the tall Bavarian wore deep lines of trouble, care and vexation. His great fist, which lay on the oaken table, opened and closed as though it were deliberating whether to give up or hold fast something; and his foot, the toes of which seemed to wish to burst the buckskin of his top-boots, stamped the unswept floor so that a cloud of dust rose up like smoke from a tobacco pipe. He struck the ground with his broadsword, and then immediately afterwards drew out of a bag of Cordovan leather, which bore the city arms embroidered in silver, a pair of heavy keys, which he seemed to try in an invisible keyhole, as though he wished to lock a door so that it could never again be opened. Then he put the key-pipe to his mouth and blew a bugle-call which he had had plenty of opportunity of learning during the long siege with its repulsed attacks and unsuccessful sorties.

Suddenly he heard a loud tread and the clanking of armour on the stairs. The burgomaster at once replaced the keys in the bag, fastened it, and swung the strap from which it was suspended round, so that it hung behind him. Then he placed himself in what looked like a defensive attitude, as though he knew who was about to enter through the door.

"Good morning, commandant!" he said to the officer who entered and threw his torn hat with its smoke-soiled plume on a seat.

"Good morning, burgomaster," returned the officer, sitting down at the other side of the table.

There followed a long pause of silence, as though two duellists were loading their pistols in order to shoot each other down. At last the commandant broke the silence by asking abruptly, "What did the Bregenzers say?"

"Not a sack of meal, not a glass of wine, till the town has given up the keys! That was what they said."

"Well?"

"Well?" repeated the burgomaster with a threatening glance.

"You won't give up the keys?"

"No! a thousand times no! a million times no!" He sprang from his chair, crimson in the face.

"Do you know," asked the commandant, "that the corpses are poisoning the city, since the Swedes took the churchyard of Eschach?"

"I know it!"

"Do you know that all the horses and dogs in the town have been killed?"

"I know it. And I know too, that my own watch-dog, my companion for twenty years, since I lost my wife and child, was the first to be sacrificed."

"Do you know that the waters of the lake have risen, that the cellars are full of water, and that no one can take refuge there any more if the bombardment is continued?"

"I know it," answered the burgomaster.

"Do you know that our vines, which are growing outside on the hills on Hourberg, in Schachten and Eichbuhl, are ripe for vintage, and that the Swedes and French are pillaging the vineyards like starlings?"

"I know it. But do *you* know that peace may be concluded to-day, that it is perhaps already concluded, and that we may save our honour if we wait one more day before capitulating?"

"One day more!" repeated the commandant. "One day more! So we have said for three months, and meantime our children are dying. Perhaps you do not know that the cows give no more milk, since they have been obliged to eat the moss from the roofs, the leaves from the trees—yes, even the dung from the horse-stables, and to lick the empty meal-sacks. It has come to that; and now the children are crying for milk."

"The children! Don't talk to me of children—to me who have seen my only daughter put to shame. Then it was I who begged for help, but in vain! To hell with the children! Why didn't you take them over the water before the Swedes had their punts on the lake?"

"You are a wild animal, burgomaster, and not a man. You would perhaps have liked to have seen them drowned in sacks or eaten, as they did in Bohemia."'

"Yes, we have become wild beasts among wild beasts during the thirty years full of slaughter and fire, robbery and whoremongering. It could be called war as long as the Swedish King lived and led 'soldiers,' but now they have become incendiaries and highway robbers, who destroy for the mere sake of destruction. Huns, Goths and Vandals, who destroy out of sheer rage, because they can produce nothing."

A cry from the street prevented the commandant's answer and drew the two out on the terrace. Crowding closely round the barrels which had been just drawn to land, some coopers were knocking their bottoms out so that the contents ran into the street.

"What are you doing down there?" called the commandant.

"Ah, it is only milk which the greedy Swiss have sent us instead of wine," came the answer from below.

A woman with a child on her arm came up, and when she saw the white stream flowing down the street, she uttered a terrible cry and placed her child on the ground to let it drink. Drawn by her cry, many other mothers came, and the babies seized the cobble-stones with their hands as though they were the softest mother's breast, and licked up the sweet milk like thirsty sucking pigs, while their mothers cursed the coarse men who thought of nothing but themselves.

"Burgomaster!" resumed the commandant, still more excited by the repulsive sight, "let us go on the roof and see what the Swedes are doing; afterwards we will talk of the other matter. As you see, all bonds are broken: one takes what another has not the power to hold; family life threatens to dissolve, and young people live anyhow; every moment one may fear an uprising."

The burgomaster did not listen to him, but ascended the attic stairs till he crept out through a garret window between the beams on to the stair-like offsets of the wall. Up these he clambered to the gable crowned by a flagstaff to which a telescope had been fastened. Underneath him lay the town in its desolation. Not a single whole roof was to be seen; not a tree was left in the old garden—they had all been used for food or fuel. Along the lake shore all the houses had been pulled down and all the gardens destroyed in order to furnish material for the ramparts. Through the streets streamed ragged, hungry, dirty men with wild gestures, all evidently on their way to the inn, "Zur Krone," round which a crowd was beginning to gather.

The burgomaster now looked through the telescope which was directed to the opposite shore. There were ranged row on row of hills, dotted over with white steep-roofed farms, surrounded by pillaged orchards and vineyards. Enclosed in the midst of them lay Eschach, where the Swedish headquarters were. An unwonted bustle was perceptible round the blue and yellow standards, and soldiers seemed to be making some preparations with the cannon which the burgomaster during the long siege had learnt to know well. He had even given the worst beasts in the first siege-battery nicknames. A great scoundrel of red copper, which had smashed the painted windows of the town church, he had named "the red dog." On the left a great mortar, known as "the blunderbuss," was a regular scupper-hole when it began to discharge its contents. "The devil's grand-mother" was the name he gave to a third, made of Swedish iron and said to be the King's own invention. And so on with the rest.

But behind the besiegers' rampart, on a garden terrace, he saw the Swedish Field-mar-shall sitting with his officers and drinking "lake-wine"—their wine which they had cultivated and vintaged and then, stupidly enough, left in the cellars on the opposite shore. As they smoked and drank the officers were studying a drawing, which, however, did not seem to be a map. It reminded the burgomaster of a rumour that Wrangel had wished to transport the Bavarian castle Aschaffenburg to his estates by a lake in Sweden; but as that was impracticable it was said that he had caused designs of the building to be drawn up by an architect, after he had first stripped it of its furniture and other contents.

The sight of the wine and the tobacco aroused for a moment the burgomaster's lower desires, which had been so long suppressed, but his hatred and his grief, which he had cherished for a generation, soon reasserted themselves. For those who had no more food nor drink, who had been deprived of everything dear to them and of peace, nothing remained but honour. By the side of his daughter whom he had himself killed (though he could not adduce this secret as a reason for his obstinacy), he had sworn that he would not give up the keys of the town as long as he was alive.

Suddenly he saw a cloud of smoke rise from "the red dog," heard a cannon ball whir over his head and then land on the road below, where it was greeted with a loud outcry.

"The keys, burgomaster, or we are lost!" cried the commandant, who had mounted the gable stairs.

"To your place, commandant, on the rampart, or you will be hung!" answered the burgomaster.

"Give up the keys, or we will come and fetch them!" roared the major.

"Come then and fetch them!" was the reply.

A number of heads looked out of the garret window, and there was a repeated outcry for the keys.

"Go down from the roof, they are aiming at us!" cried the burgomaster to the people, who began to clamber up the gable steps in order to put their threat into execution.

The next moment the flagstaff was shivered into splinters, struck by a bullet. The burgomaster turned half round and would have fallen, if he had not supported himself on his great sword. He now drew himself up and remained standing on the topmost ridge of the roof, like a stone statue on a cathedral. The people below, however, who had greeted the courageous bearing of their burgomaster with a cheer, were impelled anew by their fears to make an attempt against him, as the keys of the town were in his possession and until they were given up the formal surrender of the town could not take place.

With the help of the malcontents, the commandant ventured on a last attack against the immovable burgomaster. Accordingly he mounted to the top of the dangerous stairs, drew his sword, and demanded that the burgomaster should descend or defend himself where he stood. But it soon was evident that the latter's position was impregnable; and convinced of the impossibility of compelling him to give up the keys, the commandant turned to the people and asked them three times successively whether they accorded him the right to open the town gate and to hoist the white flag.

His question being greeted with an enthusiastic affirmative, he returned the same way as he had come to the ramparts, accompanied by the crowd.

The burgomaster, who had remained behind alone, and perceived that there was no more hope of saving the town, seemed at first to collapse, but he immediately rose up again as though he had formed a resolve. With trembling hand he opened his bag, took the great keys out, and after he had made the sign of the cross, he threw them as far out into the lake as he could. When they had disappeared in the deep waters, he fell again on his knees and with folded hands commenced a long, low prayer. He would like to have made himself deaf just now, but while he called on God and the Holy Virgin he seemed to hear the blows of axes against the city gate, through which the enemy would enter to pillage and rape, to hang and to burn.

But after he had prayed a while he became aware that silence lay over the whole town, and that the cannonade had ceased. Only from the ramparts came a low hum of voices which seemed to be speaking all together; the sound swelled louder and louder till it grew to an uproar and a shout of joy.

He rose from his kneeling attitude and saw a white flag waving from the Swedish headquarters. Then there sounded a peal of trumpets and a roll of drums which were answered in a similar way from the ramparts of Lindau. This was followed by the sound of axe strokes against the city gate. A boat pushed off from the Swedish camp and military music sounded from the opposite shore. And now a cry went through the streets of the town—at first a mere meaningless noise like the sound of waves breaking on the beach; but it came nearer, and presently he could distinguish the final word "concluded," without knowing whether it referred to the capitulation of the town or something else.

But the cry became clearer and clearer as the crowd stormed along the shore of the lake, and waving their hats and caps called up to their valiant burgomaster, "Peace is concluded!"

"Te Deum Laudamus!" was sung in the evening in the Franciscan church, while the inhabitants of the town intoxicated themselves with the contents of the wine barrels which had been brought from the surrounding villages.

When the service was over the burgomaster and the commandant sat with a jug of wine between them in the "Zur Krone'" inn. In one of the roof-beams was embedded the black bullet which had shot down the flagstaff. The burgomaster contemplated it and smiled—smiled for the first time after ten years. But he suddenly started as though he had done something wrong. "The last shot!" he said. "It is long since the first was fired in Prague—a whole generation. Since then Bohemia has lost two million men out of its three, and in the Rheinpfalz only a fiftieth part of the inhabitants remain; Saxony lost one million out of two; Augsburg does not now count more than eighteen of its eighty thousand. In our poor Bavaria two years ago a hundred villages went up in smoke and flame. Hessen laments seventeen towns, seven and forty castles, and four hundred villages. All because of the Augsburg Confession! For the sake of the Augsburg Confession Germany has been laid waste, torn to pieces, cut off from all the seas, left without air, choked, and has miserably perished. Finis Germaniae."

"I don't think it was the Augsburg Confession which did it," objected the commandant. "See the Frenchmen celebrating their Masses like good Catholics in the Swedish camp. No, it was something else."

"Well, it may perhaps have been something else," answered the burgomaster. He emptied his glass and went home to sleep quietly—for the first time after thirty years—thirty terrible years.